"I won't break into Munder's casino for three days.

"I promise you, no illegal entries, but that doesn't mean I'm going to stay away from there." Her eyes gleamed challengingly. "And don't even try to stop me."

"You think I could?" he asked.

"No. So don't waste your time."

With a quick movement he turned, gently pinning her between his hard body and the car. "I don't like the idea of you going anywhere near Munder's place."

"You don't have to like it," she persisted valiantly, trying to ignore the husky attraction of his voice. "We're playing with my cards and by my rules."

His warm breath feathered her cheek as he chuckled. "Honey, that was before I dealt myself in."

Dear Reader,

Welcome to Silhouette. Experience the magic of the wonderful world where two people fall in love. Meet heroines who will make you cheer for their happiness, and heroes (be they the boy next door or a handsome, mysterious stranger) who will win your heart. Silhouette Romances reflect the magic of love—sweeping you away with books that will make you laugh and cry, heartwarming, poignant stories that will move you time and time again.

In the next few months, we're publishing romances by many of your all-time favorites, such as Diana Palmer, Brittany Young, Emilie Richards and Arlene James. Your response to these authors and other authors of Silhouette Romances has served as a touchstone for us, and we're pleased to bring you more books with Silhouette's distinctive medley of charm, wit and—above all—*romance*.

I hope you enjoy this book and the many stories to come. Experience the magic!

Sincerely,

Tara Hughes
Senior Editor
Silhouette Books

RITA RAINVILLE
It Takes a Thief

Published by Silhouette Books New York

America's Publisher of Contemporary Romance

To Ann, Marlys, Lori and Suzanne.
You made this one easier.

SILHOUETTE BOOKS
300 E. 42nd St., New York, N.Y. 10017

ISBN: 0-373-08502-8

First Silhouette Books printing May 1987

America's Publisher of Contemporary Romance

Printed in the U.S.A.

RITA RAINVILLE

grew up reading truckloads of romances and replotting the endings of sad movies. She has always wanted to write the kind of romances she likes to read. She finds people endlessly interesting, and that is reflected in her writing. She is happily married and lives in California with her family.

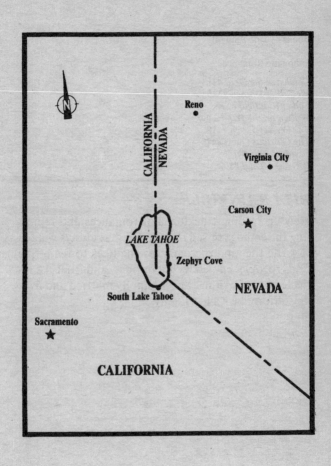

Chapter One

The first thing Dani Clayton learned that fateful night in July was that being a cat burglar was more nerve-racking than she'd expected it to be. The second was that she obviously needed a few more lessons in breaking and entering. And the third? That being caught by one's intended victim was a nasty piece of business.

But such thoughts were far from her mind as she stood at the solid oak office door of one of Carson City's casinos, listened a moment, inserted one slim piece of metal in the expensive lock, then another. Her intent expression switched to one of deep satisfaction when, after a small click, she turned the knob and the door opened to reveal an empty office. A very luxurious office, she noted with a frown of disapproval, taking in the quietly elegant room.

With neat, economical movements she closed the door behind her. A deep-piled creamy carpet absorbed the sound of her footfalls as she walked across the room to the dark chocolate, two-drawer file. Sitting down before it, she calmly selected a smaller piece of steel and slid it in the corresponding smaller lock. A faint smile crossed her face as the lock gave. She hadn't lost the knack; Nicholas's efforts over the years had not been in vain.

Dani wasn't even visibly disturbed when, after a few minutes of concentrated searching in the bottom drawer, she noticed two black, masculine shoes planted beside her outflung leg. They were polished to a state of perfection reached by only one man of her acquaintance: Nicholas. The knife-sharp crease in the expensive trousers could only belong to the same man.

"I told you I could handle this," she muttered, not even bothering to look around.

The toe of one shoe nudged her thigh as she replaced one packet of papers and reached for another.

"Stop it, Nicholas," she hissed, slipping off a rubber band and hastily shuffling through the stack of records. Rebinding them tidily, she dropped them back with a sigh of disgust and gloomily eyed the rest of the drawer's contents. There were no printed forms littering the bottom of the drawer. Nor were any arranged in alphabetical or any other order.

Despite herself, she was impressed. The owner of the elegant office and chocolate-colored file might run a crooked casino, but he was undeniably neat. However, the last thing in the world she needed right now was a neat crook, she decided. It would have made her job easier to find a drawer packed with a variety of papers.

The toe nudged her again, gently.

Resting one gloved finger on the drawer as she stared at its near emptiness, she asked absentmindedly, "If you were a contract, Nicholas, where would you be?" Curling her fingers into a fist, she tapped the side of her hand thoughtfully on the toe of his shoe. "In a safe," she decided. "That's where you'd be. Why don't you look for one while I finish going through the rest of this stuff?"

Returning to her self-imposed task, Dani muttered, "This man has a rubber band fetish. Everything in here is wrapped in at least six of them." She rolled the stretchy elastic off a small box and watched in distaste as the band squirmed and coiled messily around her fingers.

The toe moved again, as if it liked the feel of her resilient thigh. "Who's Nicholas?"

Dani dropped the box and stared at the shiny drawer handle. *Who was Nicholas?* Only the man who had taught her all she knew about the art of burglary—and definitely not the one who was asking the question.

"Who's Nicholas?" repeated the deep, slightly gritty voice that was nothing at all like the dry, amused tone of her mentor. "And who are you?"

Slowly Dani turned and craned her neck. She looked up a long way, past the black, creased trousers, past the matching formal, hand-tailored jacket and crisp white shirt, to a stubborn-looking chin and dark eyes that didn't give an inch. I'm a lady who's in big trouble, she decided after a moment of deep thought.

Her gaze swung back to the file drawer. She prodded it with a finger and watched as it silently slid back in place. If this were a movie, she thought, all I'd have to do is stall for a while and the cavalry would come charging to the rescue. But it wasn't a movie, and there would be no cavalry. The only one who even knew she was here was Nicholas, and she had told him she could handle this little project herself. He would be sitting at home, waiting for her to return. However, stalling didn't seem like such a bad idea. In fact, with her options suddenly whittled to nothing, it was her *only* idea.

Sighing sharply, she swung around to face the silent man. Following an impulse, she bent her knees and held up her hands. One of his large, tanned hands joined hers; the other scooped up the small case resting on the floor beside her. Then, effortlessly, he pulled her to her feet.

Her five-foot-five frame came up to his chin, which meant he was about six feet, Dani reflected, silently looking up at him. Unfortunately it looked like six feet of disapproving questions and fast reflexes. His expression was even less comforting; it was as implacable as the planes of his face. He wasn't handsome, she thought, taking advantage of his cool assessment to continue her own. He was too tough to be considered good-looking.

His thick hair was a deep, tobacco brown, a few shades lighter than his eyes, and was brushed straight back in a fairly conservative cut. It was as disciplined as his mouth. His neatly trimmed mustache and straight brows were the same rich brown. He reminded Dani of the lean, lithe, dangerous cowboys in her favorite old Westerns.

After a long moment he stepped back with smooth grace and waved her to a comfortably upholstered amber chair. Her brows rose as he seated himself between her and the door.

He leaned back and stretched his legs out, unconsciously preserving the knife-sharp crease in his pants. "Who are you?" he asked for the second time.

"Danita Clayton. Who are you?"

"Rafe Sutherland. This is my office," he added negligently. His eyes never left hers in the silence that followed. Trying not to squirm, she waited.

"Now why don't you tell me about that contract?" he asked in a far too gentle voice. It didn't match the look in his eyes. At all.

Actually, she decided the last thing in the world she wanted to do was explain. He knew too much already. Hadn't she even suggested that he go look for a safe? But that was all he knew and she wasn't about to tell him any more. Besides, how could she tactfully explain that she was driven to such extremes because he was a crook? That if his casino hadn't been littered with rigged games, her best friend's husband wouldn't have lost every penny he had, plus signing the equivalent of a five thousand dollar IOU? An IOU he couldn't redeem. And that without this particular chain of events, she wouldn't have remembered the old maxim that it takes a thief to catch one? Nor would she have optimistically thought that a quickie refresher course with Nicholas would solve the problem.

She mentally counted her blessings. Yes, there were a few. He hadn't turned her over to a goon squad. Yet. He hadn't even called the police. Yet. And while he *was* making sure she didn't run for the door, he hadn't threatened her. Yet.

Rafe Sutherland gazed unblinkingly at the composed woman before him, his shuttered expression concealing his racing thoughts. What was he going to do with her? He didn't need a lie detector to convince him that she was no run-of-the-mill thief. No thief at all, if his instincts were running true to form. But she had broken into his office, and now she had the gall to sit there with a proud tilt to her head, looking as if he had brought an unpleasant odor into the room with him. The expression in her hazel eyes was frankly disapproving.

One lean hand held up the wallet-sized case of lockpicks for her inspection. "You realize that merely possessing these trinkets could get you a state-subsidized vacation for several years? If you tack on the fact that you broke into my office and rifled my files, you're talking about a long time out of the Nevada sun."

Dani leaned forward, her eyes alight with sudden curiosity. "You knew I was in here, didn't you?"

Rafe nodded.

"How?"

"Our TV picked you up as soon as you stepped into the hall."

Dani considered his statement thoughtfully. "Why didn't someone stop me?"

"I wanted to see what you were up to."

"Where were *you*?"

Rafe's dark gaze never shifted from her face, although it did linger momentarily on her deliciously slanted, almond-shaped eyes. "In the security office. Watching you pussyfoot down the hall and fiddle with the lock." His expression grew grim. "If I hadn't been there, your reception would have been . . . different."

Dani blinked. The pause before his last word conjured up images of burly men with businesslike guns breaking down the door and hauling her out of the office. "Why did you let me get in?"

He shrugged. "No reason not to. I don't keep any money in here. Or financial records. I wanted to know what I had in here that was worth stealing." He watched her attempt to control her expressive face before adding, "I'm still waiting."

You'll wait until hell freezes over, she thought, sliding down in the chair until she was resting on her tailbone. Her lashes lowered, obliterating the hard face before her.

Rafe leaned back, idly turning the leather case in his hands. She wasn't going to make it easy. He scowled, eyeing her from head to toe. In her dark jeans, black, ribbed turtleneck and dark sneakers she looked like a kid dressed as a Hollywood version of a cat burglar. Except she was no kid. Probably twenty-four or five. And soft. With a delicate pointed chin that was undoubtedly stubborn and a mass of light brown hair that was piled on top of her head and held there by some feminine bit of magic.

"Danita, unless you would prefer talking to the police, you'd better sit up and open those cat eyes."

Something in his voice stiffened her spine. Involuntarily her lashes lifted. She looked at him in amazement. This man, this...*crook*, was actually threatening her.

"I don't think you really want to call in the police," Dani said slowly. "After all, people who live in glass houses shouldn't go around lobbing stones." She noted the startled expression in his eyes and leaned back in satisfaction.

"Would you mind translating that cryptic statement?" he asked, turning the leather case over in his hands. His voice was casual, but Dani saw that his knuckles had whitened.

"It seems obvious to me," she said with a shrug. "With all that stuff you must have out there—" she nodded toward the front of the building "—rigging your games—"

"What?"

"I don't think you want the police nosing around."

Dani watched the man's features tighten. It was an intimidating process, and the look he cast her was enough to singe the fuzz of her sweater. She wasn't being deliberately foolhardy, she reminded herself. She simply didn't have that much to lose. If he had been an honest businessman he would have turned her over to the police. But he hadn't. Ergo he was crooked as the hind leg of a rabbit. Therefore the only leverage she had at this point was a little blackmail.

"What the hell are you talking about?"

"Relax," she soothed, averting her eyes from his fierce expression. "I'm not trying to get you to say anything incriminating. Look." She held out her arms. "No tape recorders, no bugs. I'm just saying if you let me go, you won't have the police coming too close to your...ah, operations."

"What operations?" His voice was as grim as it was demanding.

"Your *crooked* operations," she said with asperity, realizing that euphemisms were wasted on the man.

"Lady, you do have your nerve," he said in wonder, taking a deep, calming breath. It obviously didn't have the desired effect, because when he spoke, his voice was icy with anger. "And not a shred of self-preservation. If I *were* running rigged games, the next time your loving family saw you, it would probably be beneath several inches of dirt and a tall cactus."

"How you can deliberately cheat people is beyond me," Dani said heatedly, losing the last bit of control over her impulsive tongue. "Taking food out of their mouths and clothes from their children. How can you sleep at night?"

"Easily," Rafe replied, his eyes gleaming with interest. He was intrigued by his first glimpse of the woman behind the intrepid facade. Impetuous, caring, and fiercely protective of someone. Fascinating.

"Do you have any idea how many poor souls are in debt because of people like you?" Dani asked, mounting her favorite soapbox.

"None," Rafe said promptly, sternly controlling a grin at her impassioned attack. "If you hadn't been so busy breaking in my back door, you might have noticed my clientele."

"Thousands!" Dani informed him, waving a hand wildly and answering her own question. "Thousands of people bankrupt and without credit—all because of gamblers like you."

"Wrong." Rafe spoke before she could catch her breath. "I don't gamble, and my patrons are well heeled. They can afford whatever they lose."

"They come here on vacation, planning to spend a few bucks on slot machines. Before they know it, they're over their heads in debt."

"Not at my place. It's a private club. No one just walks in here off the street."

"There ought to be some way to control the vultures who prey on innocent people."

"There is. The Nevada Gaming Commission. Fortunately, the Golden Door has a reputation—well deserved, I might add—for running a clean house."

"You should hear some of the horror stories I deal with. People who—" Dani stopped as if she had run into a wall and looked at him, a frown creasing two lines between her brows. "What did you say?"

Rafe thought a moment. "The Nevada Gaming Commission?"

"No." She waved her hand impatiently. "After that. What did you call this place?"

"The Golden Door."

"Are you sure?"

Rafe looked at her. The urgency of her question and the horrified expression on her face answered his most urgent question. "Reasonably. It's been in the family for years," he said quietly.

"Oh...my...God," Dani muttered, appalled. "You're positive? It isn't the Golden Boar?"

"That particular bit of sleaze," he informed her in a hard voice, "is a couple of blocks down the street."

Dani closed her eyes and slumped back in the chair. "Nicholas is going to have my head for this."

"Who's Nicholas?"

One eyelid opened, revealing a baleful, hazel-green eye. "Must you keep asking that?"

"Just until I get an answer."

The eyelid dropped back down, displaying ridiculously long brown lashes. "I can't believe it," she groaned. "I broke into the wrong place."

Rafe silently observed her chagrin. Her hair broke loose from its casual topknot, cascading over the deep gold fabric, highlighted by the lamp at her side. He controlled the urge to reach out and touch it. Instead he repeated the question.

With a sharp sigh Dani said, "Nicholas is the man who taught me everything I know about opening locks and all the stuff that goes with it."

"I think you need another teacher," Rafe said, and watched a scowl draw her brows together again.

"I didn't say he taught me everything he knew," she said between clenched teeth.

"What is he?" Rafe asked in irritation. "Some fagin who sends you out to steal for him?"

Hazel eyes froze him, and at that moment Rafe decided that while she might be a woman who knew very little about self-preservation, she obviously rated top marks when it came to unswerving loyalty and devotion.

"Nicholas is a member of my family," Dani said in an icy voice that literally begged him to start an argument.

"Then he should take better care of you," Rafe replied, giving in to the irresistible temptation.

Dani sat up and took a deep, infuriated breath, stretching her sweater to its capacity. "He does," she informed him frostily. "Usually. But this time I convinced him that I could handle things. And believe me," she added gloomily, "he's really going to be ticked." She stared down at her sneakers, absently poking the toe of one into the deep pile of the carpet. Then she looked up with a dawning grin. "On the other hand, he's the one who told me how to get in here, so he can't get too mad."

"What *is* this?" Rafe asked, disbelief spreading over his face. "Am I on everybody's hit list all of a sudden?"

Dani waved a calming hand. "Only because of a stupid mistake. Nicholas misunderstood the name of the casino and did research on this one."

"He didn't do a very good job. We picked you up on our scanner as soon as you opened the door."

Dani sighed. "That's because I didn't come in the way he told me to." She studied his suddenly alert expression. "You know that single window on the fourth floor?"

"Nobody could get in that way," he said flatly.

She sat patiently, waiting until he was ready to listen. "Nicholas did. Last night. He made a dry run. He even won a few dollars at your blackjack table before he left. Out the same window."

Rafe's eyes narrowed in concentration. "If it was so easy, why didn't you come in the same way?"

Dani sighed again. "I don't think I have the patience to be a good burglar. It looked like it would take too long. The door was too tempting."

Definitely not a thief. A gleam of satisfaction shimmered briefly in Rafe's dark eyes. "I still want to know what you're doing here. Why don't you start at the beginning?''

Dani glanced at her watch. "That would take forever."

"All right, then start with Nicholas."

"That's almost the beginning," Dani objected. She waited for Rafe to say something, but he just sat, waiting.

"When my parents got divorced," she began abruptly, "Mom turned our big old house in Los Angeles into a bed and breakfast."

Rafe blinked, sternly controlling his surprise. Danita Clayton was obviously a woman who took things literally.

"Before long, the B and B turned into a permanent residence for several older people."

"How many?"

"Five."

"And?"

"Nicholas was one of them. He and the others became my family."

Rafe spoke quietly, watching her expressive face. "What line of work was Nicholas in?"

A smile tilted the corners of her mouth. "He was a cat burglar."

"Ah."

"Not just any cat burglar," she informed him proudly. "Before he retired he was the best."

"Did he announce his retirement today?" Rafe inquired pleasantly.

"No, years ago," Dani said in surprise. "Oh, you mean last night?" At his nod she explained carefully, "He gave up *burglary* a long time ago, but he still can't resist the challenge of locked doors and tight security measures. He just likes to drop in on people," she finished weakly in the face of his unencouraging expression.

"His profession must have been a surprise to the others," he finally commented.

Dani's small smile was noncommittal. She decided not to bother explaining that the others had been too involved with their own lives to be concerned about Nicholas. Billy Bob Norton, for instance, had been busy bridging the gap between life as a small-time Oklahoma rancher and overnight oil millionaire. Tabitha McGary was an animal trainer with a live-in orangutan, Zak, who kept life in a constant state of upheaval for everyone. Arthur Marlow, retired stock-broker and Wall Street whiz, was the quietest of them all. Emily Pinfeather, who looked like a stereotypical grandmother, was actually an ardent crusader who traveled the country, leapfrogging from cause to cause. No, they had not been disconcerted by Nicholas's nocturnal habits.

Dani checked her watch again.

Rafe ignored the gesture. "You haven't told me how you got involved in this whole thing. Why are you helping Nicholas?"

"It's the other way around. Nicholas is helping me."

"Why? How did you get mixed up with a bastard like Jed Munder?"

"I've never met the man," she equivocated.

"You're in this thing up to your eyeballs," he said flatly. "Why?"

Dani's sigh was one of pure exasperation. "Look, this is a long story and has nothing to do with you. I'm sorry I broke into your office by mistake. Why don't you just accept my apology and forget the whole thing?"

Good question, Rafe thought. Why didn't he? The last thing he needed was to get mixed up with a fledgling burglar. He had enough on his hands at the moment. But he was also strangely reluctant to let Danita Clayton walk out the door. "I like long stories," he said lazily.

Dani glanced imploringly at the ceiling. When no response was forthcoming she gazed at the man settled in the high-backed chair before her. He looked as if he had taken root. He obviously wasn't planning to move until she satisfied his curiosity.

"My best friend's husband came here on a weekend trip with some friends," she said abruptly. "He walked into the Golden Boar to look around. Jim had never done much gambling and was fascinated by the noise and glitter. Somehow or other he got snookered into a game of blackjack. He won a little at first, but in a couple of hours he was in big trouble."

Her voice tightened as she went on. "He asked for credit, got it and kept on gambling, hoping to win enough to get out of the hole he was in. Instead he just dug it deeper."

"Naturally."

Dani glared at the matter-of-fact statement. "Finally, in order to leave with all of his limbs intact, he signed some ridiculous contract. It stated that the kindly Mr. Munder had loaned him five thousand dollars, which he would repay, with interest. Exorbitant interest."

"Of course."

Her hands tightening into fists, Dani said, "You needn't sound so smug."

"Not that. Just . . . not surprised. Anyone in town could tell you that's how Munder operates."

"Too bad Jim didn't meet someone in town before he went in the place," she said bitterly.

"I still don't understand what you have to do with his problems," Rafe said, assessing her taut body and clenched fists.

Dani looked at him in surprise. "He came to me for help."

"Why?"

She shrugged. "Everyone does."

"Why?"

"Because I help them."

"Why?"

She stared at him thoughtfully. "Because I can't stand to see people in trouble. Especially if I can do something about it."

It figured, Rafe thought, closing his eyes in resignation. She was a bleeding heart if ever he saw one. Probably everyone she came in contact with took advantage of her.

"And what did you think you could do about it?" he asked carefully.

"Break into the crummy place and steal his contract." Her expression said *that* should have been obvious. "If they had no contract, no hard evidence, they couldn't hold him to anything."

Rafe grimaced and shook his head pityingly. "That's the most naive—and stupid—thing I've ever heard."

Dani heard the defensiveness in her voice as she said, "Well, Jim couldn't think of anything, and that's the best I could do."

"Munder doesn't do things legally, Danita. He might not get his money, but he'd make sure it was taken out of your friend's hide."

"Well," she said after a thoughtful pause, "I'll just have to think of something more effective." She cast a third look at her watch. "But right now I have to go home."

Rafe stood. "I'll drive you."

"No need to do that. My car's downstairs."

"I'll have it delivered to you tomorrow morning," he promised.

Dani held out her hand for the leather case. Rafe turned his back and locked it in a drawer of the huge walnut desk.

"I may need those," she objected.

"Tough."

There was a remarkable lack of sympathy in his voice, she reflected. Ah, well, if she had to, she could always break in and steal them.

Rafe touched her shoulder and gestured to the door. "Ready?"

He had a stubborn expression on his face that warned her she was going to be taken home despite any protests she could conjure up.

She shrugged. "If you insist."

Once he closed and locked the door, she tucked her arm through his and said, "On the way home, you can tell me all about Jed Munder and his infamous Golden Boar.''

''Why?'' he asked, distrusting her rapt, wide-eyed expression.

''I need all the information I can get.''

''Why?'' he repeated grimly, drawing to a halt and clamping a hand on her shoulder to hold her still.

Her brows rose in surprise as hazel eyes met dark ones. ''Because now I have to break into *his* place.''

Chapter Two

The hell you do!"

Dani glanced over at the scowling man sitting beside her. He had been saying that, in one form or another, ever since they'd left his office. He had stated it quite calmly as they walked down the hall, muttered it as they passed the tuxedo-clad man at the door and snarled it through clenched teeth as he stuffed her in his silver car and slammed the door. Now, leaving the city lights behind them as they drove north into the valley, he was not inhibited by the presence of his clientele or staff.

"You're not to go within a city block of that place. Do you hear me?"

Rafe wasn't yelling. He didn't have to, Dani thought. He loaded enough menace in his low-toned statements to kill off a herd of wild boar. The only problem with his adamant position, she reflected, was that this whole thing was absolutely none of his business. Whatever the issue, he didn't get a vote. Now all she had to do was convince him of the fact.

"Where are we going?" he asked, following her pointing finger and making a right turn.

"Way out of town on a country road that ends at a rambling Victorian house."

"Is that where you're staying?"

"Well, actually, no. That house is where my mother's lived for the past six months since she married Brady. I'm staying at the Victorian about a mile this side of it."

"Brady Cameron? The photographer?"

"Um-hmm. Know him?"

"I met him and his wife, Sara—"

"My mother," she amplified with a satisfied nod.

"About a month ago at some civic affair. Nice couple."

The man was certainly not given to exaggeration, Dani thought with an inward smile. They were more than nice—they were terrific. They had been married less than a year, and they were so much in love they almost tripped the light switches when they walked into a room.

"So why are you staying at the other house?"

"Because Mom and Brady are on a trip and I'm staying with the family. It's a place they all bought when they moved out here from L.A. about a year ago." And if she was lucky, they'd all be in bed by the time Rafe got her home. He had already dealt with a burglar in his office and that was enough for one night. She had a gut-level feeling that he wasn't ready for an infatuated, possessive orangutan. Or a suspicious cowboy. Or, for that matter, an anxious and irritable burglar, a vague stockbroker, an outspoken animal trainer or a crusader who was momentarily without a cause.

Luck, she noted with a fatalistic sigh when they finally pulled into the driveway, was not with her. But, considering what the evening had already dealt her, she wasn't surprised. Lights blazed from the windows as if the inhabitants had never heard of monthly electric bills or an energy crisis. And, despite the fact that she was opposed to gambling—on general and any other kind of principle—she was willing to bet that they were all hovering behind the door, just waiting to pounce.

"Thanks for the ride," Dani said hastily as Rafe removed the key from the ignition. "Don't bother getting out. And thanks for being so understanding," she added belatedly, remembering that if he had reacted differently she would probably now be explaining a dicey situation to the police. She held out her hand, intending to end the evening with a business-like handshake, just as Rafe turned away and opened his door.

"I'm not understanding," he stated evenly, meeting her at the front of the car and tugging a dress Stetson down over his forehead. He touched her elbow and steered her to the walk leading up to the front porch.

"Do you have to wear that?" she asked with a frown, looking up at the white hat.

"Yes." The word was a flat statement of intent. He had apparently humored her enough for the evening. The hat was not negotiable.

Dani shrugged as well as she could with one arm shackled by his large hand. He couldn't know that Zak, an orangutan with a penchant for western hats, was waiting on the other side of the front door. Or that Zak would steal the hat at the first opportunity. She should probably explain, she thought with a weary, inward sigh, glancing up at him. One look at his grim expression changed her mind. His patience had obviously been tried too far already. Besides, who would believe a jumbled explanation of an almost human ape who was a movie star and who had recently added being a pickpocket to his list of handy skills?

"Nor am I kind," Rafe continued evenly, ignoring her interruption. "If you want to be grateful for something, make it the fact that I'm curious."

"Curious?" she asked, dragging her heels as he tried to hustle her up the stairs.

"Exactly. I want to meet the man who encourages you to break into casinos and the family that apparently gave its seal of approval."

"What makes you think they did?" She drew to a halt several feet from the door.

"Did any of them try to stop you?"

Dani shook her head, gazing up at him. Of course they hadn't. They had known that she would be perfectly safe as long as she followed Nicholas's directions.

The door was thrown open just as she reached for the knob.

Rafe *did* have quick reflexes, she thought a moment later, remembering her initial impression in his office. Her own were a bit slower. Of course, she hadn't expected him to take one startled look at the opening door, utter a pithy Anglo-Saxon expression and spin her behind him, she rationalized.

He stiffened until his back felt like a chunk of granite, his only movement a deep breath that lifted his shoulders and fed oxygen to a body preparing for violent action. Resting one hand on his taut, muscular shoulder, she peered around him.

A hulking form stood framed in the doorway, a lamp from the room highlighting the orange hair covering its body. Two long arms reached up, grasping the lintel. Then one lowered and touched the wall beside the door. The porch light beamed on, and Rafe sucked in his breath, absorbing the sight of an openmouthed orangutan fiercely displaying its large, stained teeth.

"Hi, Zak," Dani said weakly after a quick glance up at Rafe's frozen expression. Nudging him with an elbow, she muttered, "He's harmless, but don't mind if he's a little abrupt. He's been acting strange lately. I think he's got a crush on me." She opened the screen door and walked in, accepting a noisy, affectionate kiss on her cheek from the ape. Looking back over her shoulder, she missed the possessive glare Zak directed at the man behind her. "Are you coming in?"

Rafe stepped forward, automatically removing his hat. His fascinated gaze never shifted as the ape shambled forward, its knuckles brushing the gleaming oak floor. Dark, beady, hostile eyes examined him. Then one long-fingered hand was extended in a grudgingly courteous gesture, waiting to take his hat. The ape's gaze, now frankly covetous, dropped to the snowy Stetson.

"No." Dani's urgent call stopped Rafe just as he was about to surrender his hat.

He jerked it back, glancing at her, then down at Zak just in time to catch the frustrated gleam in Zak's eyes.

"If you give it to him, you'll never see it again," Dani said. "Don't let him touch it." Turning back to the sulking simian and pointing to the man beside her, she said, "Zak, this is Rafe, a friend. Understand?" Moving her fingers quickly in the sign language she had learned with Zak, she repeated, "*Friend*, Zak. And keep your mitts off his hat!" Then, satisfied that she had stopped whatever mischief was brewing, she moved lightly across the entry hall.

Rafe kept a wary eye on his new friend. Zak waited until Dani's back was turned, then pursed his lips and stuck out his tongue in a silent raspberry. Apparently satisfied by that display of temperament, he returned and slid his hand in Rafe's, silently urging him to follow Dani. With one hand clutching his hat and the other firmly attached to Zak, Rafe shrugged and went along, wondering what other surprises awaited him in the next room.

"I'm home," Dani announced, stopping with Rafe and Zak in the doorway.

A slim, aristocratic man looked up from the newspaper neatly folded in quarters on his lap. A cup of coffee steamed gently on the table beside him. His comprehensive glance took in the wry look on her face and the expressionless man standing behind her. "You didn't get it," he stated.

"No." Dani shook her head slowly. "I got caught, instead."

"How did you go in?"

Trust Nicholas to get right to the heart of the matter, Dani thought. "The back door," she admitted.

A small, whipcord-thin man with a weathered face interrupted. "That was a damn fool thing to do, darlin'. What would your mama say if she knew you weren't paying attention to Nick here?"

"Her mama would have all our heads if she found out we hadn't talked Dani out of the crazy idea in the first place," stated a commanding feminine voice.

"Did you get a look at their accounting system?" a tall, bony man with a shock of white hair asked. At her negative reply, he lost interest and picked up another magazine from the stack on his lap.

A plump pigeon of a woman sitting in a high-backed chair with her ankles neatly crossed spoke up. "I said all along that this wasn't the way to go about it. What you need," she added complacently, "is some leverage. Then you apply pressure."

Rafe studied the group as five voices spoke at once.

"When I give you directions, I expect you to follow them."

"Dani, darlin', when you're dealing with a ring-tailed bastard like that, you gotta keep on your toes."

"Maybe you should have used Zak to create a diversion."

"You should have gone for their computers."

"I can organize a demonstration. All I need is twenty-four hours."

With an ease that bespoke years of experience Dani acknowledged the comments with a nod and turned to the man beside her. "Rafe, I'd like you to meet the family." She performed the introductions, and Rafe mentally sorted them all out.

Nicholas had the silver-shot brown hair and dark eyes. He also had a subtle sophistication that would allow him to blend in with the highest level of society. Billy Bob Norton wore cowboy boots and had the look of a man who'd grown up on a horse. When he looked at Dani his light blue eyes were filled with fierce love. Tabitha McGary was a gray-haired wisp of a woman with a voice that could stop a herd of rampaging elephants cold. Arthur Marlow, judging from his reading material, was a computer nut. Emily Pinfeather had a peculiar shade of brown hair, obviously dyed, and her eyes were hazy with thought. She was probably already planning an alternative approach for Dani, Rafe thought.

"And, family, this is Rafe Sutherland, the man who caught me robbing his office and decided that I'd be safer at home."

Five pairs of eyes silently scrutinized Rafe. He carried the whole thing off pretty well, Dani decided. It couldn't have been easy. He was still looking for somewhere to place his hat, and Zak, eyeing the Stetson with longing, was sticking to him like glue. After several long, assessing glances the men rose and shook hands with Rafe.

"Here," Billy Bob said gruffly, reaching for Rafe's hat. "I'll take care of that for you. I've had a lot of practice keeping things away from that cross-eyed, bowlegged, hairy runt." He joined Tabitha at the game table, with Zak hard on his heels.

Dani dropped down on the floor in front of Nicholas and waved Rafe to a nearby chair. Crossing her legs tailor fashion, she said to him, "Pull that closer to us." She looked up at the older man and grimaced. "Okay, Nicholas, say it."

Rafe leaned back, studying the other man, then shifted his gaze to Dani's expressive face. He stopped in silent appreciation when he reached her hazel eyes. They were wide, intriguingly tilted at the corners and extravagantly framed in dark brown lashes. Her shining mass of hair fell in soft waves around her shoulders, and he realized with annoyance that he had an overwhelming urge to thread his fingers in it and comb back the strands that strayed across her forehead and around her cheeks.

She wasn't beautiful, he thought, struggling to remain objective. Her mouth was probably too wide, her chin too pointed. But somehow those minor flaws were lost in the overall impression of intelligence, humor and subtle feminine allure. No, not subtle, he decided with characteristic honesty. Not at all. She sat on the floor, covered from neck to toes in stark black, and should have looked as prim as a nun. Instead her soft curves were outlined against the moss green rug, gracing her with staggering sensuality. He swore silently as hunger, as unexpected as it was sudden, ripped through his body and settled heavily in his loins.

Nicholas neatly folded the newspaper and set it aside. "What happened?"

Dani told him, starting with her reason for selecting the door instead of the window and ending with the ride home. It was a fair accounting, Rafe concluded, seeing another aspect of the woman before him. Her report was well organized, concise and objective. She didn't gloss over her mistakes. When she finished she sat quietly, looking up at the old man.

He leaned back, steepling his fingers and looking through them to a distant point. "So," he added with a thoughtful frown, "I told you how to get into the wrong place?"

Dani patted his knee. "Not to worry. I probably told you the wrong name."

"It was careless of me," Nicholas said, his frown deepening. "I should have known your friend couldn't just walk into the Golden Door. And he certainly wouldn't have found slot machines there."

"You don't spend your time in casinos," she reminded him. "How could you know?"

"I should have found out before I let you go there," he stated evenly. Turning his attention to the rest of her story, he asked briskly, "Well, what did you learn?"

"That I'm good with lockpicks, but I don't have the patience to deal with small details," she said promptly.

His brows shot up. "You call going in the wrong way a small detail?"

"Or the bigger ones," she amended with a slight smile.

"Ah."

After the extended silence Dani shifted impatiently and asked, "Now what? How am I going to get Jim's contract?"

"You aren't," Nicholas said in a no-nonsense voice.

"Nicholas."

He waited until her anguished protest died down, then added, "I'll take care of it." After lifting the cup of coffee to his lips and taking a swallow, he said, "You can come with me, but just remember that this time I'm in charge."

Rafe stiffened, disbelief spreading across his face as everyone spoke at once.

"When can we get started?" Dani asked, flashing a brilliant smile.

"But this time, darlin', you damn well better listen to Nick."

"Sara's going to kill us all," Tabitha stated.

"If I go along, I could break into their computer file," Arthur mused.

"You need a diversion," Emily informed the room at large.

Zak stared longingly at the white hat.

Dani ignored the others. "What about tomorrow night?"

"Hold it," Rafe said, breaking into the jumble of voices. "You don't just walk into a place like that, pick up what you want and walk back out. He's got—" He broke off. Not one person in the room was listening to him. All six of them were still talking at the same time. Make that five, he amended silently. Nicholas was calmly drinking his coffee, totally ignoring the babble of voices.

Rafe rose. "No one is going to the Golden Boar," he said determinedly. When the voices broke off into startled silence he said calmly, "You're going to forget the whole thing."

Six faces turned to him in polite inquiry. After a moment five of them turned back to Nicholas and the stream of advice resumed.

Rafe didn't wait for their momentum to pick up again. "If you don't, someone's going to get hurt. Jed Munder plays a particularly nasty game of hardball." And he didn't want Dani Clayton's fetching little body anywhere near the action, he realized with a sudden jolt.

Dani looked up in annoyance. It had taken her long enough to talk Nicholas into this particular scheme, and the last thing she needed was someone throwing cold water on it. She was pleased that Rafe hadn't turned her over to the police, but she was not so grateful that she'd let him ruin her plans. "Don't you have somewhere to go?" she inquired with an appalling lack of tact.

"No." Rafe dropped back in his chair, never even rumpling the crease in his pants, she noted with disgust. "I seem to be the only voice of reason here," he added. "And I'm going to keep talking until *someone*—" he looked directly at Nicholas "—listens to me."

Five voices broke out in protest, clamoring until Nicholas raised a quelling hand. "I think he deserves to be heard."

Rafe looked at the circle of mutinous faces, sighing audibly. "You have no idea what you'd be up against at the Golden Boar. First of all," he said flatly, "I don't think the place is vulnerable. Munder's security system is reported to be the best."

Nicholas raised an interested brow and murmured, "Really?"

Ignoring the dry query, Rafe added carefully, "His staff is handpicked to . . . handle difficult problems."

Dani watched as his expression grew hard. "You mean they're *gangsters*?" she asked after a long pause.

Rafe shrugged. "Probably."

"That's a heck of an attitude. Why isn't someone doing something about it?"

"Someone is," he assured her.

"Who?"

"A group of casino owners."

"Including you?"

He took his time about answering, she noted. Pulling words out of him was as hard as distracting Zak when he had his eye on a Stetson.

"Yes," Rafe admitted reluctantly. "And, believe me, we don't want a bunch of well-meaning amateurs getting in the way."

"*Amateurs?*"

Rafe stopped Dani's outburst with an upraised hand. "What do you call your performance tonight?"

"That has nothing to do with what we're talking about!"

"It has everything to do with it," he replied in a hard voice. "Just where do you think you'd be right now if you had been caught in the Golden Boar?"

"That's not—"

"Where?"

"Probably beneath several inches of sand and a tall cactus," she admitted, repeating his earlier words with a frown.

"Right." He matched her scowl with one of his own.

"Nicholas isn't an amateur," she muttered, glaring up at him.

His hard gaze swung to the older man. "Nicholas wasn't the one I caught in my office," he reminded her.

Nicholas spoke for the first time. "She won't be going out on her own again."

"She shouldn't be going out at all."

Five pairs of eyes settled on Rafe, considered his implacable expression, then swerved to Nicholas.

"She won't do anything rash," he promised.

Rafe was not comforted. Their definition of the word obviously differed from his. As far as he could tell they were all ready to plunge headlong into a volatile situation, heedless of the danger involved. Ignorant of the danger involved, he amended silently, studying their faces.

The challenge, as he had expected, came from Dani.

"What are you and your local chamber of commerce group doing about it?"

Selecting his words carefully, he said, "We've been working on this for several months now. Will you trust me to handle it?" Knowing it wasn't enough, he read the answer in her eyes before the words formed on her lips.

"Sorry," she said, shaking her head slowly. "With my friend's future—possibly his life—on the line, I can't. Your mysterious approach may take forever, and he needs help right now." She glanced at Nicholas, exchanging a long look with him. Turning back to Rafe, she said, "We'll try not to interfere with your plans."

Not moving from her position on the floor, she watched as Rafe rose and strode to the far end of the room. He stopped in front of a large window and stared, unseeing, into the darkness beyond the front porch. Then he turned slowly, his dark gaze shifting to her.

Dani slowly drew in a quick, stunned breath, absorbing his blatant masculinity. Was she blind, she wondered, not to have noticed it before? Earlier, he had merely been someone who had caught her in an awkward situation and was big enough and strong enough to prevent her from attaining her goal. Later, he became annoying, persistent and determined. And now? In an aggressive, wide-legged stance with his fists resting on his hips and his unbuttoned, dark jacket hooked behind his wrists, he was as impressive as he was intimidating. A sudden premonition shimmered through her as she eyed his stubborn chin and go-to-hell eyes. He was, she acknowledged gloomily, going to complicate her life something fierce!

"The men I'm working with," he began abruptly, "have been...concerned about Munder and his casino for some time now. We've managed to get someone inside his place to—"

"Act as a spy?" Emily asked, entranced.

"Collect information," he said repressively. "I don't think I need mention that if word gets out, the man is as good as dead."

Six heads nodded in acknowledgement. Zak nodded amiably along with the others, sliding one hand near the snowy Stetson on the table.

Billy Bob scowled and moved the hat closer to Tabitha.

"We need evidence," Rafe continued. "Good, solid evidence—and lots of it. This is the only way we see of putting him out of business."

"How long has your man been in there?" Nicholas asked.

"Just over a month."

Dani leaned back against a floral sofa. "And how much longer do you think it will take him?"

"Three days at the most."

"That's all?"

"Three days," Rafe repeated.

Dani glanced sideways at Nicholas and met his gaze. He moved his shoulders in a lazy shrug. "I gave myself two weeks," she said slowly. "That's how much time Jim has until the walls come crashing in." She looked up at Rafe and nodded. "We'll give you three days."

"No breaking and entering during that time?" he pressed. "No spur of the moment midnight flits? No costumes?" He eyed her dark clothes thoughtfully. "Or sleight of hand with locks?"

Dani shook her head disgustedly, seeing her options being drastically reduced.

"You'll stay completely away from there for the next three days?"

Her head stopped moving and she said, "No."

"No? What do you mean, no?" Rafe demanded, walking over to stand in front of her.

She held up her hands and waited until he tugged her effortlessly to her feet. From that vantage point, she only had to look up a short distance to meet his eyes. "I agreed that none of us would break into the place and look for Jim's contract, even though it would be a piece of cake for Nicholas," she informed him, refusing to be intimidated by his narrow-eyed scowl. "But, just in case your plan doesn't work, I'm not eliminating all of my options. I reserve the right to wander in there and look around. In fact," she added with a small smile, "all of us have been curious about that place. We might be coming and going a lot in the next few days."

The sharp sound of a hand connecting with the table cut short Rafe's exasperated sigh.

"No! You red-haired son of a baboon, get away from the hat! Tabitha, tell him to leave it alone!"

"Leave it alone, Zak," she said obediently.

"You could put a little more feeling behind it," Billy Bob muttered, grabbing the Stetson and handing it to Rafe.

"I'll walk out to the car with you," Dani said, not giving Rafe a chance to find another resting place for his hat.

After a chorus of good-nights and a slight smile from Nicholas, Rafe opened the screen door and walked down the steps to his car. "You're in an awful hurry to get rid of me," he complained mildly to the woman beside him.

"Not at all," she said briskly, lying through her teeth. "I just thought Zak was getting too close to that sparkling white hat."

He stopped, leaning against the fender of the car. "I think I can manage to keep at least one step ahead of an overgrown monkey."

"Ape," she murmured. "Monkeys have tails. And don't be too sure about that. Zak is no ordinary, household variety ape. He's been trained for the movies and has a lot of tricks up his nonexistent sleeve."

"About that promise you made," he began, draping his arm around her shoulders and tugging her against his long frame.

Dani stiffened, rejecting the drugging effect of his lean muscles and warm body. "Three days," she reminded him. "No illegal entries for three days, but that doesn't mean I'm going to stay away from there." Her eyes gleamed challengingly. "And don't even try to stop me."

"You think I could?" he asked, his eyes narrowing with interest.

"No. So don't waste your time."

With a quick movement he turned, gently pinning her between his hard body and the car. "I don't like the idea of you going anywhere near Munder's place."

"You don't have to like it," she persisted valiantly, trying to ignore the husky attraction of his voice. His hands settled on the bare skin of her rib cage beneath the dark sweater, and she jumped like a skittish colt. In a distracted voice she repeated one of Billy Bob's favorite dictums. " 'We're playing with my cards and by my rules.' "

His warm breath feathered her cheek as he chuckled. "Honey, that was before I dealt myself in."

Chapter Three

Early the next afternoon Rafe pulled up in front of Dani's place, a gorgeous Queen Anne tower house of cream and terra cotta, accented with touches of olive green and dark brown. He hadn't been able to see anything beyond the lighted porch the night before, so he took his time, admiring the craftsmanship of earlier generations.

He took the stairs two at a time and crossed the wide, wraparound porch, heading for the front door. Before he had a chance to ring the bell Tabitha's authoritative voice stopped him.

"Dani's around back. In the greenhouse." Her encompassing gaze took him in from his gleaming brown boots and western-cut slacks to his light blue chambray shirt and buff Stetson. "You sure like to live dangerously, don't you?" she asked, indicating his hat with a nod. "Wearing that, when you know you're going to be around Zak, is flat out asking for trouble.''

"Actually,'' he said with a small grin, "I came to see Dani, not Zak.''

Tabitha shrugged. "Same difference. When you see one, you see the other.'' She slid to the side of the glider swing and motioned for him to join her.

"Why is that?'' he asked, settling down beside her.

"They share a lot of history. They practically grew up together, learned sign language together, and even though Dani only gets up here on vacations, they always pick right up where they left off.''

"I've seen his movies,'' Rafe commented. "They're good. Have you always been his trainer?''

Tabitha nodded. "I got Zak when he was just a baby. But Dani's helped me a lot over the years, doing the time-consuming stuff, drilling him until he got a sequence just right.''

"Did she work on that Western where he played the piano and picked pockets?''

Smiling reminiscently, Tabitha shook her head. "No, I had to do that one without her. She was setting up her business in L.A. during that time.''

Rafe looked down at the small woman with sudden interest. "What kind of business?''

"Hasn't she told you?''

Tilting his hat to the back of his head and resting one arm behind her on the frame of the swing, he said, "So far, the only thing I've learned about her is that she has more courage than good sense. But I plan to find out a lot more.''

"Good luck,'' Tabitha said, standing up with a brisk movement. Moving toward the door, she added,

"Don't count on it, though. You've already got one big strike against you."

"What do you mean?" Rafe asked, regarding her with a puzzled frown.

Studying Rafe's curious expression, Tabitha sighed inwardly. Pity, she thought, he was just the type she would have chosen for Dani. Her gaze dropped to his muscular shoulders and narrow hips. Yes, he was undeniably attractive, and somewhere beneath all that hard-headed determination, if that grin was any indication, lurked a lively sense of humor. Things would never be dull for them. Ah, well, she thought optimistically, it still might work out. She wouldn't give up. Not just yet.

Aware that he was waiting, she explained succinctly, "Dani doesn't like gambling. Or anyone connected with it."

Rafe's brows shot up. So the lady had strong objections. Interesting. That explained the disapproving gleam in her eyes as she'd lectured him on the evils of gambling the night before. Mulling over Tabitha's statement, he rose and followed the brick walk around to the back of the house.

The large, two-story greenhouse was all glass and wood beams, a tasteful and charming addition to the house. The windows were lined with banana trees. As he approached the door he heard Dani's voice raised in amused protest.

"Zak, you're cheating!"

Rafe entered and closed the door behind him. He waited, concealed by the foliage, and watched the scene before him. A large, circular trampoline stood in the center of the room. A platform had been erected near one rounded edge, and above, long, cable-thick ropes hung from the wooden beams. Dani and Zak were taking turns on the ropes, pushing off from the platform, swinging out over the trampoline and returning to their starting place. Zak was guilty as accused. He was indeed cheating. Each time Dani swung out, he would tug at the bottom of the rope, slowing her down.

"You'd better watch out," she told the ape between short bursts of laughter. "I know how to stop you."

Dani wore a white knit shirt and shorts. She obviously took advantage of the California sun, because every visible square inch of skin was a warm shade of honey. To Rafe, standing silently by the door, she looked good enough to eat.

"All right, I've had enough of this nonsense," she said, dropping lightly to the platform and gesturing for Zak to take off. Grinning, she watched him throw his weight into a wide swing. He quickly picked up height, then cautiously changed position until he was upside down, hanging by one arm and leg. Each time he passed Dani, he teasingly reached for her hair or attempted to plant a kiss on her cheek.

"Okay, Zak," she called, ducking his smacking lips and watching him swing away, "now you've done it. This is it!"

Carefully studying his trajectory, she extended her arm and aimed at him. Raising her thumb and sighting down it, she pointed her forefinger and yelled, "Bang!"

Zak clutched his heart, let go of the rope and dropped like a stone. He was as stiff as a board when he hit the trampoline, flat on his back. He rose in the air, toes and nose up, then hit and bounced twice more, never breaking his pose. Finally, when he couldn't milk any more bounce or drama from the situation, he sat up and grinned at Dani.

Rafe applauded softly as he moved away from the door. "Well done."

Dani turned slowly, stopping when she saw him silhouetted against the light coming through the glass door. "Hi," she said warily, trying to ignore the sudden thudding of her pulse. "I didn't see you. How long have you been there?"

"Not too long." But long enough to recognize the affinity between her and the ape. Long enough to appreciate her slender legs, sweetly curving hips, small waist and high, firm breasts. Long enough to regret the end of the impromptu show, the cessation of her supple movements.

Zak scooted to the side and swung down to the floor. Dani dropped off the platform, bounced a couple of times, then sat down, her legs dangling over the edge of the trampoline. Before she could move Rafe wrapped his hands around her waist.

It would have been a simple matter for him to ease her to the floor, she thought later. Instead he lifted her and drew her to him, allowing her to slide down the length of his warm body until her bare feet came to rest on the floor between his shiny brown boots.

"Uh, you can let me go now," she finally said.

After a charged pause he asked, "Do I have to?"

Distracted by an urgent tug at her knit shirt, Dani looked down. Raising her eyes to meet Rafe's, she said, "Yes, I think so. My buddy here has no trouble at all cracking coconut shells with his teeth. Do you really want to risk having him take a chunk out of your leg?"

Rafe glanced down beyond Dani and met hostile, beady eyes. Reluctantly he dropped his hands and stepped back. "I thought you told him I was a friend."

"He's not stupid," she replied, running an affectionate finger down Zak's head and between his eyes to the tip of his nose. His eyes slowly crossed as he followed the path of her finger. "I introduced you that way, and he took the statement at face value. But now I think he's beginning to have his doubts. As far as Zak is concerned, a friend is someone who brings him a bag of fruit or gives him a hat," she told him, glancing quickly at the Stetson perched on the back of Rafe's head. It was definitely *not* someone who held her in his arms the way he just had, she added silently. Nor someone who looked at her the way Rafe was, sending a sizzling message even Zak could interpret.

Zak put an end to the discussion by taking Dani's hand and leading her outside. Rafe followed. Zak led the procession over to an ancient, leafy oak. Dropping Dani's hand, he pulled himself up to the broad crotch of the tree and ventured out on a sturdy limb, where he all but disappeared from sight. Dani gestured to a bench beneath the tree and sat down. Rafe removed his hat and joined her, dropping the hat between them.

Dani slanted an oblique glance at the silent man beside her. He was an enigma, she decided. After last night she didn't know what to think. To begin with, he could have caused her a lot of grief; instead he'd extracted a long and probably tedious story from her, listened with apparent interest, then brought her home. His reaction to the family had been interesting. A less determined man might have retreated. Instead he had stayed, and, for the first time she could remember, an outsider had actually prevailed against the combined forces of her unconventional honorary grandparents.

He had won the three days' grace he'd requested, so what did he want now? she wondered. Was he back to ask for additional time, or was he playing policeman, making sure she didn't go near Munder's place? Frowning at the idea, she decided Rafe Sutherland was going to have to learn that gaining one concession wasn't tantamount to winning the war.

"Mr. Sutherland," she began coolly, "I—"

"Why so formal, Danita?"

Dani blinked in irritation, then persevered. "Mr. Suther—"

He leaned back and closed his eyes. "You *do* remember my name?"

Did the man think she was a complete nitwit? Her answer came from between clenched teeth. "Yes."

"Then use it," he said lazily.

Pointedly ignoring him, Dani gazed up at the gracious old house. The formality of earlier generations had something in its favor, she thought. A restraining influence, if nothing else. And, if her reaction to him the night before was any indication, she needed all the restraint she could muster. Because she wasn't about to get involved with a man whose profession was one to which she was categorically opposed.

Keeping her voice brisk, she said, "All right, Rafe, what can I do for you?"

"Go out to dinner with me tonight."

"You drove all the way out here to ask me that!" she exclaimed in disbelief. "That's crazy! Why didn't you just call?"

"Because it'd be too easy for you to say no over the telephone. Besides, I wanted to see you."

Dani's gaze narrowed in speculation. "Why?"

Before he could answer an acorn dropped down neatly into the folded crown of the Stetson. A second one followed right on its heels. Rafe glanced up, then dropped his gaze to the woman beside him, lifting a questioning brow.

Dani nodded. "It's Zak. He has a cache up there."

Rafe looked back up, then shrugged philosophically. "It's better than having my hat stolen, I guess." After one final glance he returned to the subject at hand. "Are you always so suspicious?"

"Ordinarily, no," she said after a moment's pause. "But when dealing with a man like you—one, by the way, who's made no bones about the fact that he wants me out of his hair—yes. Definitely."

"A man like me?"

His voice was smooth as silk, Dani reflected, if you discounted the slight edge that accompanied the words. "A gambler," she explained courteously.

Rafe stretched out his legs, leaned back and turned his face up to the sun. "Tell me about your experience with gamblers."

Dani eyed him warily. His calm voice urged her on, *lured* her on. It invited her unguarded tongue to lead her right into a trap of his making. Warily she said, "I don't know any personally."

"You know me," he pointed out.

"Not really."

"I'm working on it," he assured her lazily. "So tell me about the gamblers who blighted Uncle Willie's life."

"I don't have an Uncle Willie."

"Whoever. Something must have happened to someone you care about."

"To a lot of them."

Rafe sat up, studying her militant expression. "A *lot*? What do you do, go out and beat the bushes looking for victims?"

"I don't have to. They come to me." Something flickered in his dark eyes. Anger? Exasperation? Whatever it was, he quickly controlled it.

Ignoring a broken chain of acorns hitting his hat and rolling down to settle in its brim, he said in an even voice, "I'll bite. *Why* do they come to you?"

"Because it's my job to help them."

She watched that look return to his eyes. She couldn't really blame him, she decided. From his point of view her verbal foot-dragging must seem like deliberate provocation. But it wasn't that at all. She was just oddly reluctant to discuss her work with him. Probably because she expected him to make some remark about a patsy, a soft touch, or whatever its equivalent was in the state of Nevada.

Without moving a muscle Rafe seemed to settle down on the bench as if preparing for a long winter. It was amazing, she reflected, how much he could communicate without uttering a single syllable.

Finally, after a deep sigh, he asked, "Your job? Could you narrow it down a bit? Give me a clue?"

"I'm a credit counselor."

Dani watched a few more acorns hit the hat and roll around the brim while Rafe thought. He shoved his hands in his pockets and looked at her, eyes narrowing in concentration. She could practically see his brain computing, analyzing and deducting. It didn't take him very long.

"I never would have guessed. How did you get involved in something like that?"

Now *there* was a question! And it wasn't one she particularly wanted to answer. It wasn't really any of his business that she had once been a credit card junkie, using plastic cards with the abandon of a chocaholic running through a candy factory.

The corners of her generous mouth tilted in a smile as she remembered. The day of reckoning had eventually come; she'd finally take an objective look at her mounting pile of bills, another one at her paycheck, and realized that she was up to her eyelashes in debt. No, it had not been the best of days. In addition to the fact that she had practically been facing bankruptcy, she had felt like an absolute fool. She had lived with Arthur Marlow, a financial wizard, most of her life and apparently not one jot of fiscal sanity had brushed off on her.

She had turned to Arthur for advice and got an earful. He expounded on the deceptive high-interest rates and intricacies of easy credit. Arthur talked at length, painting a thoroughly depressing picture of overextended credit and the triple whammy of using conventional credit cards, revolving credit and installment loans. After that, when it was obvious his lecture had made an impression, he offered several suggestions. The first one was that she sliver and trash her credit cards, keeping only one for emergencies. The second was that she prepare a realistic budget, and the third was the offer of a loan, with a reasonable interest charge, so she could repay her bills.

The traumatic experience changed her life. After reducing her own debt load, she'd realized that many of her friends were in the same situation. Most of them hadn't been in over their heads because they indulged themselves, they were simply attempting to maintain an ordinary standard of living in the face of double-digit inflation. And they all eventually made the same discovery: when using cash advances from credit cards to pay for the necessities of life, it was no simple matter to cut down on spending. She had returned to Arthur, seeking a solution. What she found was a new profession.

Arthur was not an impulsive man. Following his usual method of operation, he considered all available data. She was, he told her, ticking off the facts on his fingers, one of life's givers; she was most satisfied when serving others. Not in a subservient position, mind you, but coming from a position of strength, from which help could best be dispensed. Her recent ordeal had left her empathetic to others in the same position. Her current job with the film industry might be interesting, but it was a dead end and hadn't even tapped her potential. Ergo—Arthur was big on ergos—it was time to consider a new, challenging career. He, of course, had a specific suggestion—one he had been considering for a long time. If she approved, he would train her and provide her with a start.

He had done exactly that. In addition, he had mentioned the project to Billy Bob and gained additional financial backing. Some months later, she had emerged as a qualified consumer credit counselor, prepared to manage a nonprofit financial counseling service.

A tap on the shoulder brought her out of her reverie.

"Your job," Rafe prompted, intrigued by the varied expressions chasing across her face.

"I help people with their finances," she said, opting for the least complicated explanation.

"And gambling makes your job harder?"

"Right. Of course," she added honestly, "credit cards are the biggest problem, but when my clients are gamblers, I have to work twice as hard."

A wry smile twitched his mustache. "Why do I have the impression that you get involved in a lot more than their fiscal matters?"

"I can't imagine," she said, widening her eyes in mock-innocence.

"It might be because I found you rummaging through my office. That wasn't exactly the act of a deskbound pencil pusher."

She nodded after briefly considering the matter. "You've got a point."

"Are you always that accommodating?"

"Hardly." It wasn't a lie, she decided. Yes, she did a lot of things that he would consider above and beyond her job description, but certainly not *always*. "Anyway, this was different. Jim is married to my best friend, and they have two little girls. Four lives could be ruined by this crook, and I just wasn't going to let that happen."

She sensed his skepticism and wondered why she was bothering to explain. "Later, when I thought about it, everything just fell into place. It was too perfect to pass up!" She turned to face him, absently scooping up several acorns. "Don't you see? The casino was in Carson City and so was Nicholas. I knew he'd help me. So I just packed my bags and came."

Rafe watched her toss an acorn into the air. A long-fingered hand, followed by a long, hairy arm, reached down and snagged it in midair. "You were so sure he'd get involved in something this risky?"

"Of course." It was a simple statement of fact.

"Why?"

"Well, in the first place, it wouldn't be risky for him. In the second—" Dani paused, carefully selecting her words "—Nicholas has always been there for me when I needed him. And third, he gets bored when things get too quiet. So, in a way, I was doing him a favor."

She glanced up and saw that Rafe was speechless. Before he could recover she hurried on. "I think I mentioned that he retired from the criminal stuff a long time ago, but he enjoys little sorties like this."

"He doesn't consider breaking and entering illegal?" Rafe asked, his face expressionless. "I don't think the police would agree with him."

"It's a moot question," she said thoughtfully, "because he's never been caught."

"Besides, this time he let you run the risk."

Dani jumped up, brushing against the hat and causing a stream of acorns to hit the ground. Frosty hazel eyes considered him as she said, "I explained that last night. I'm not going through it again."

Zak peered through the leaves, saw his prize nuts bouncing in all directions and swung to the ground. Grumbling, he crouched and retrieved them.

Rafe stepped around the busy animal and reached for Dani's hand. He lifted it, cupping it in his. Touching her soft palm, then closing her fingers over it, he said, "You've got those five people curled up right here, don't you?"

"I guess I do," she replied slowly. "I never thought about it that way. But if I do, it's reciprocal. I love them all, and there is nothing that I wouldn't do for them."

Rafe's dark eyes assessed her solemn expression; then he mentally added staunch support and unquestioning assistance to the list of attributes he had begun cataloguing that night in his office. He already knew that she wasn't overly concerned about legalities; her outlook was apparently quite elastic. Measured against love or compassion, the law came in a poor second. Dani Clayton offered herself unconditionally to those she cared about. And, he realized, he very much wanted to become one of that select group.

"No!" Dani leaped back to the bench and snatched Rafe's hat out from beneath Zak's hand. Zak jumped guiltily, then with a quick, unconvincing shrug that indicated total disinterest in the hat, reached for the last few remaining acorns on the bench seat.

"I don't mind if he touches it," Rafe commented, watching the byplay with amusement.

"Bite your tongue," Dani said, handing it to him. "Two minutes of his tender loving care and you wouldn't even recognize it. And at the going price of those things, I refuse to reimburse you for damages. So consider yourself warned."

With a quick tug at the brim, Rafe settled the hat low on his forehead. He dropped his hand on Dani's shoulder and turned her toward the house. Shortening the length of his stride to match hers, he said, "About tonight. Where do you want to eat?"

Dani sighed. The man obviously didn't know the meaning of the word "rejection." If he didn't get what he wanted the first time around, he'd just keep hammering away. Someday, someone was going to teach him a much needed lesson. However, she admitted with another sigh, it wasn't going to be her—at least not today, not over something as minor as a dinner invitation.

"Here," she said.

Rafe drew her to a halt, his dark gaze probing her expression. "Here? Why?"

"Because—" she waved her hand in a gesture that included all the inhabitants of the house "—they're all going to be gone tonight, and I offered to baby-sit Zak." Seemingly aware that he was the object of discussion, Zak reached out and firmly grasped Dani's hand before looking up to scowl at Rafe.

"Everyone?" he asked, startled.

Dani nodded. "Even Mrs. Mallory. The cook," she added in response to his mute question. "Can you barbecue a medium-rare steak?" she demanded, wondering how he would look dodging smoke, with a little barbecue sauce splashed on his immaculate clothes.

"I can." The question was, did he want to? For once in his well-ordered life he wasn't quite sure what his plans for the evening or the enticing Miss Clayton had included. The only thing he was absolutely certain of was he did not want to spend the next few hours being glared at by a jealous, irate ape who could crunch coconut shells between his teeth.

"Of course, there's always tomorrow," Dani said cheerfully, noting his restraint, waiting for him to produce a smoothly voiced excuse.

One look at her expectant, wide-eyed expression and the decision was made. What the hell, he thought. He wanted to know what made Dani Clayton tick, didn't he? What better way than to spend the evening on her home turf? "I like my steak rare," he said.

Dani's smile slipped. After a thoughtful pause, she said, "Why don't we see what Mrs. Mallory left us to work with?"

Dani obviously considered cooking a challenge, Rafe concluded a few minutes later. One that she approached with verve. She had already pulled every variety of green known to man out of the refrigerator and was now ready to pounce on anything else that would add crunch and color to the salad. She washed, peeled, diced and shredded with abandon, leaving a trail of multihued remnants littering the sink and tiled counter.

If it were anyone else concocting that mess, he thought with stoic wonder, his appetite would be ruined. Dani, however, intrigued him. In spite of the abomination she was creating. He found himself wondering if she approached all aspects of her life with the same haphazard enthusiasm. Did she, he mused, give herself to a man with such unself-conscious warmth and spontaneity?

Dani slanted a quick peek up at Rafe. He was staring at the contents of the crystal bowl in fascinated horror. He must be one of those purists, she reflected, tossing in a handful of diced jicama, who considers a leaf of lettuce and a cherry tomato a salad. "Are you into cooking?" she asked, attempting to distract him as she added a few garbanzo beans.

"I'm into whatever it takes to fill an empty stomach," he replied, blinking as she sprinkled some finely sliced purple cabbage into the bowl.

"How do you feel about desserts?"

"Eating them?" he asked, as she reached for cheddar cheese and a grater.

"Making them," she said succinctly. Flourishing the grater, she added, "you can have the run of the kitchen." Whatever it took to keep him from breathing down her neck and eyeing everything she reached for with tacit disapproval.

Out of the corner of her eye, she watched as he finally moved away, quietly opening drawers and cupboards. Rafe took a folded dish towel and tucked it around his waist, securing it behind his belt. Next, he placed a whisk, bowl, shallow pan, measuring cups and spoons and long-stemmed goblets on the counter next to hers. Well, she reflected, he obviously wasn't going to settle for Mrs. Mallory's homemade peanut butter cookies.

He also looked as though he knew what he was doing. He assembled eggs, sugar and cream, located the liquor supply and returned with bottles of amaretto and tangerine liqueur. Dani edged closer to his work space, cheese drifting from the grater to the counter.

Rafe's large hand closed over her wrist, stopping her. With his other hand he gestured to the sink between the two countertops. "See that line?" he asked, pointing to the center of the double sink. Dani looked, noting his pristine area and her own war zone. She nodded.

"Good," he said, releasing her wrist. "Cross it and you're dead."

Chapter Four

Rafe did know what he was doing in a kitchen, Dani thought later as she hesitated, weighing the merits of adding pickled beets to the salad bowl. She watched him as he worked with silent precision. And he did it very well, she reflected. He was neat, organized and systematic. He had whisked a week's worth of eggs, sugar and liqueurs in a bowl before setting the mixture in a pan of simmering water, patiently lifting the whisk until a thick ribbon formed. Then he'd whipped the cream and remaining ingredients without splattering a drop.

"What's that?" she asked, watching as he combined the cream with the base and spooned it into the goblets. If asked, she would deny it to her dying breath, but the simple elegance of the mixture reminded her of the man who was so absorbed in its preparation.

He shrugged, adding a dollop to the last glass. "Zabaglione, or a variation of Bavarian cream. Whatever you want to call it."

A slight frown drew her brows together. "Isn't it a little, uh..." she began.

Rafe carefully covered the goblets, then transferred them to the refrigerator before he looked up. "A little what?"

"Well..." She paused, searching for a tactful way to put it. Finally, giving up diplomacy as a lost cause, she said, "Plain?"

His gaze slid from her earnest expression to the overflowing salad bowl.

"I've got some chocolate chips you can sprinkle over the top," she offered.

"No, Dani," he said in a tone that should have ended the discussion.

"Granola?" she said hopefully. Before he could reply she reached for an overhead cupboard, "I know Mrs. Mallory has some pretty little gumdrops in a jar up here."

Rafe shook his head.

"How about a little drizzle of chocolate syrup? Or a spoon of peanut butter? Sliced bananas?"

"Nothing," he said. Observing her discontented expression, he added wryly, "Think of it as adding a touch of austerity to your life."

She turned and regarded the salad in brooding silence. Finally, sprinkling some poppy seeds into the bowl, she muttered, "You act as if my life is an unbroken chain of impetuous, extravagant events."

What else would you call a life-style that considered breaking and entering a perfectly reasonable solution to a client's financial dilemma? Rafe wondered, amused. Wisely opting to remain silent, he tore off a sheet of plastic wrap and offered it to Dani, hoping to distract her from the bowl of salted peanuts she was contemplating. She reached for the plastic absently, covered the salad and stowed it in the refrigerator.

"How did you get into the credit counseling business?" Rafe asked later with genuine interest. They had finished their dinner and were lingering at the table over cups of coffee. The salad, he'd discovered after a tentative bite, was good, an interesting blend of flavors and textures. It merely served to whet his interest in its creator.

"Why are you so intrigued, or should I say surprised, at my choice of profession?" she asked, placing her cup in its saucer and leaning back in her chair. She fingered the empty goblet idly. He had been right, she decided. Even one chocolate chip would have been sacrilege.

"Somehow it just seems out of character," he said slowly. "I can't see you spending your days bending over a desk, balancing rows of figures for people." In fact, he decided, given the fact that her business tactics were as flamboyant as her taste buds, it was a wonder she hadn't been forced into bankruptcy before the first payment was due on her office furniture.

Regarding him thoughtfully, she finally said, "You're right, it is out of character. Or was. In school, math was never my strong point. I couldn't even balance my own bank account until Arthur took me in hand."

"So how did it happen?"

Dani added hot coffee to both their cups, replaced the glass pot and leaned back, gazing over his head.

After a moment she said, "It all began with my first credit card."

Carefully selecting her words, she gave him a drastically edited version of her financial history and how she came to have Arthur as her professional mentor.

"Did he think you had an aptitude for fiscal matters?" Rafe asked, resting his elbows on the table.

Dani grinned at his dubious tone. "Arthur had more confidence in the whole thing than I did," she admitted cheerfully. "He's of the opinion that there's no such thing as a mathematical bonehead. He insisted that I wasn't lacking in ability, I was merely disinterested." She lowered her lashes, momentarily distracted by the movement of his broad shoulders beneath the chambray shirt. "As it happened," she added quickly, bringing her straying thoughts back to the business at hand, "he was right. He was a fantastic tutor and, of course, he knew what buttons to push to get me motivated."

Rafe stared down into hazel eyes sparkling with humor and intelligence. People, he decided. Whatever else moved Danita Clayton to action, her concern for her friends, clients and the world at large was the key to her personality. And given her outlook and close association with Nicholas, it was no wonder that she moved with such facility from credit counselor to cat burglar. Looking at it from her point of view, it almost made sense.

"Actually," Dani said, standing and reaching for the plates, "I surprised myself. I turned out to have a real knack for the whole thing."

Rafe reached for the silver and cups. "And now?" he asked, following her into the kitchen. "Are you good?"

Dani set the dishes on the counter and turned to face him. A small, satisfied smile curved her lips. "I'm terrific," she said calmly.

The next day, just at dusk, Rafe looked down at the petite, gray-haired woman at his side and knocked at Dani's door. Zak, decked out in a gold braided doorman's hat, threw open the screen door with a flourish, baring his teeth. Rafe blinked, wondering if that was Zak's version of a smile or if the ape was preparing to take a chunk out of him.

"Good heavens," Elise Sutherland said faintly, moving closer to her son.

"I warned you," Rafe reminded her.

"So you did," she agreed, eyeing Zak dubiously as he shambled closer, grinning up at her.

Dani stepped from the parlor to the entry hall, calling, "Who is it, Zak?" Her voice died away at the sight of Rafe in a dark blue suit that made her aware of every masculine muscle and sinew, a white silk shirt and a discreetly striped burgundy tie. After an appreciative moment, her gaze slid over him and settled on the attractive woman who barely reached his shoulder. Neither could ever deny the relationship, Dani reflected, taking in gleaming dark eyes, peaked brows and a remarkably feminine version of Rafe's determined chin.

While Rafe performed the introductions the two women frankly assessed each other, obviously liking what they saw.

"I hope you'll forgive us for not calling," Elise said with a faint smile, reaching out to touch Dani's hand. "We can't even use the excuse that we were in the area. I made Rafe drive all the way from town."

"Because you like Victorian houses?" Dani asked dryly, amusement at Rafe's wary expression highlighting the gold flecks in her hazel eyes. He was eyeing his mother as if she were a particularly volatile explosive about to go off.

"Because I was overwhelmed by vulgar curiosity," Elise admitted. "I had to meet the woman who broke into Rafe's office." Dark eyes gleaming, she confided, "I've been fascinated by cat burglars ever since I saw Cary Grant in that wonderful movie *To Catch a Thief.*"

Rafe closed his eyes in resignation.

"Then you'll love meeting the real thing," Dani promptly assured her with a grin. "Nicholas is always delighted to meet someone interested in his profession."

"Profession?" Rafe inquired, opening his eyes just in time to move his buff Stetson away from Zak's long fingers.

Dani nodded. "Retired," she reminded him. "These days," she said, turning back to Elise, "he just does it for his own amusement."

"You mean," Elise said in utter fascination, "he still goes on, ah, *capers*?"

Rafe groaned, and Zak patted his shoulder sympathetically, stretching one gray finger to touch the brim of the hat.

Dani's brows rose in mild amusement. Rafe had apparently given his mother an expurgated version of their encounter and was now obviously sorry he had said a thing. Her gaze swept over the elegant woman clad in a simple black dress that discreetly suggested designer labels and an unlimited cash flow. Elise Sutherland, who could—and probably did—grace the pages of Carson City's society section, was a cat burglar groupie, Dani decided, a glimmer of a smile settling on her lips. And her son did not approve.

Welcome to the club, she thought. There wasn't one single person in the house, including Zak, of whom he *did* approve. He considered everyone there indulgent, foolhardy, or larcenous. And he just might have a point, she admitted fairly.

With that uplifting thought, Dani waved toward the parlor and said, "Come meet the family, Elise."

Rafe experienced a definite feeling of déjà vu as he stepped through the parlor door. Four people were speaking and one, Nicholas, was listening.

"I know some pretty high rollers," Billy Bob said. "We could pool our cash and break the bank at Munder's place."

Tabitha shook her head. "What we need is some excitement while Nicholas and Dani break in. Zak started a riot in a department store in his second movie. How about something like that?"

Arthur sighed in disgust. "I keep telling you that we can ruin the man if someone infiltrates his computers."

"I can get my Save the Whale people here from California in twenty-four hours," Emily said placidly, looking up from her crocheting and peering over her granny glasses.

Nicholas, immaculate as ever, rested his head on the high back of a blue velvet Queen Anne chair. His dark eyes gleamed as he looked around, following the various threads of conversation. If his expression was any indication, he was highly entertained.

Rafe wasn't. His expression grew grimmer with each comment. These people! They had given him three days in which to resolve the problem of Jed Munder, and they were reneging before the second day was over!

"What's going on?" he demanded.

Five faces turned to him, then shifted to the petite woman standing between him and Dani. An intrigued expression crossed Nicholas's face as he slowly rose.

Aware that Rafe was holding a tight rein on his temper, Dani hastily introduced Elise. Nicholas extended his hand to her, smiled and calmly plucked her from between the two younger people. He seated her in the chair next to his, inclined his head toward her and ignored everyone else in the room. Elise, Dani noted, did not object. In fact, she seemed enchanted with the whole thing.

Rafe cast a sharp look at them before he repeated, "What's going on?" Looking around the room, he met four blank expressions and watched four sets of eyes studiously avoid his own. He turned to the fifth. "You gave me three days."

Nicholas glanced up at the grim tone, his dark brows arched. "Merely a strategy session," he said placidly. He raised his hand, palm out, as Rafe opened his mouth. "Just in case Plan A doesn't work. You'll have your three days." Turning back to Elise, he resumed his low-voiced conversation.

Slipping her arm through Rafe's, Dani tugged and led him from the room. She couldn't have accomplished that particular feat if he hadn't cooperated, she realized. It wasn't just his size; Rafe simply wasn't a man who was easily swayed or moved. If he yielded, it was because he chose to.

Separating him from the others was the safest thing to do, she decided, leading him out to the front porch.

He was obviously in no mood to listen to the creative brainstorming taking place behind them. Also, their absence gave four of her conspirators the freedom to continue plotting their frontal attack and Nicholas the opportunity to develop something entirely different.

"They can't even wait three lousy days!" Rafe exploded as Dani sank down on the glider and pushed it back with the toe of her sandal. She patted the seat beside her. "Did you hear the things they were talking about?" he demanded, pacing the width of the porch. "*Whales*, for God's sake! And Billy Bob would like nothing more than to organize a posse with his cronies and to storm into the place on horseback," he ended in disgust.

"Don't give him the idea," Dani pleaded faintly, closing her eyes at the thought.

The swing squeaked and skittered to one side as Rafe dropped down heavily beside her. "Damn it, Dani, I'm serious. Were you *listening* to them? Their crazy schemes could get someone killed!" He frowned, staring out over the porch rail. "And it could just be the man I've got inside Munder's place."

"They won't do anything," Dani said soothingly, lightly touching his hand. "They'll talk and come up with outlandish ideas. Nicholas will listen and, for the most part, ignore them."

"What makes you so sure of that?" Rafe's tone expressed his doubt as clearly as if he had painted the words on the wooden planks of the porch.

"That's just the way they are," Dani said with a small shrug. "They each have their own areas of expertise, and they never interfere. Billy Bob might read something in the paper about some bears designated as an endangered species. He'll tell Emily, then stand back and watch her swing into action. Or Emily might think of a new trick for Zak, but she lets Tabitha do the training. Or—"

"I get the idea," Rafe said dryly. "But, considering what's going on back there—" he nodded toward the parlor "—they don't have the same hands-off policy about Munder's place."

"Well," Dani said after a thoughtful pause, "I suppose it's because *I'm* the one who brought the whole thing up, so they think of it as open territory."

"Terrific."

"But in the long run," she assured him, wanting to erase the black look from his face, "they know that Nicholas is in charge."

Rafe looked down at her earnest expression and wondered why he wasn't reassured. Then he heard a burst of laughter from the parlor and knew. "Dani, this thing is a lot bigger than your friend's debt. There's a lot at stake here."

The note of urgency in his voice brought her gaze back to his face. Leaning back against his arm, she wondered if he would ever tell her any more of his plans. Talk about bare bones, she thought ruefully. All she knew was that he and a mysterious group of associates had the "situation" in hand. And, of course, that he wanted her to keep her nose out of things. Lifting her feet, she let his long legs control the swing. There was a limit to a person's being strong and silent, she decided. And she had reached it. Idly she wondered what sort of an ultimatum she could issue. If it weren't a matter of honoring a commitment for another thirty-six hours, she could threaten to turn the household loose on Jed Munder. And that was exactly what she would do in less than two days.

"I haven't told you the scope of this thing," Rafe said abruptly. "Mainly because others are involved."

"And you took a vow of silence," she said helpfully.

Rafe surged to his feet, almost unseating her. "This isn't fun and games, Dani," he said, his voice matching the grim expression on his face. "It hasn't been for months, and until our man comes out of Munder's with the data we need and his skin intact, it won't be over."

"I'm sorry, Rafe," Dani said, cursing her quick tongue. "I have this fatal habit of making bad jokes at inappropriate times."

"Do you want to hear this or not?" he asked wearily.

She nodded.

"Munder bought his casino about three years ago," Rafe said. He leaned against the wooden post and absently slid his hands into the front pockets of his pants. The sides of his unbuttoned jacket were hooked behind his wrists, exposing a wide expanse of white silk shirt. "Right from the start, he wasn't satisfied with the house percentage, and it didn't take long for word to get around town."

"Why didn't someone do something then? Why wait until now?" Dani asked.

"We tried. Unfortunately the state gaming commission works with evidence and witnesses. We haven't been able to get either."

Dani watched as he paced back and forth in front of her, frustration evident in every step he took. "Who's we?"

"Some other casino owners and me."

"Why couldn't you?"

"Because he's not stupid. He covered his tracks too well. And his victims are like your friend. They have families, and they were properly terrorized. Some of them complained, and we heard about it, but none of them is willing to sign a formal complaint or appear in court as a witness."

Dani rose and moved over to stand by Rafe. Resting her hands on the porch rail, she waited for him to continue. When he didn't, she muttered angrily, "It's really disgusting when the law protects someone like that."

There was a distinct pause before Rafe said, "Yeah."

She looked up, alerted by something in his voice. Turning, she leaned back against the rail, watching him in unblinking silence. Finally she said, "What you're doing *is* legal, isn't it, Rafe?"

He looked out across the yard, his glance following the muted lights illuminating the curve of the drive.

"*Isn't* it?"

He stood unmoving, concentrating on the small domes of amber light.

"Rafe?"

He remained silent.

A low gurgle of laughter broke the sudden stillness on the porch. "I don't believe it," Dani said, looking up with narrowed eyes, trying to decipher his expression in the dark. "You're breaking the law," she accused in sudden certainty.

A reluctant half grin curved his lips, tilting one corner of his mustache.

Her brows rose. "Is this the man who just a couple of days ago delivered a stirring lecture on the ethics of breaking and entering?" she asked no one in particular. "The same one who had some pungent comments about a certain member of my family? Nahhh," she answered, thoroughly enjoying herself at his expense. "Pretty soon he'll explain that he's an undercover agent for the IRS. Or that he's an honorary member of the county sheriff's office."

Rafe braced himself, waiting with a surprising degree of anticipation for the hell she was undoubtedly going to raise.

"Or maybe he finds Nicholas's line of work more fascinating than he'll admit," she pondered aloud slowly. "Or is it a new type of business management class?" She directed her last question at him.

Rafe took his time about answering. "Sometimes," he finally said, "certain situations call for extreme action."

"Really?" she inquired sweetly, thoroughly annoyed at his reply. "That's precisely what I attempted to explain the other night in your office. If I remember correctly, you didn't buy it."

Dani pushed herself away from the railing, her light blue sundress washed to white by the darkness. It brushed her knees with each agitated step as she paced back and forth in front of him. "You are a most annoying man," she informed him in a clear voice. "The other night you actually had the gall to tell us that *yours* was the only voice of reason. Jed Munder played a nasty game of hardball, you said. What we were talking about was dangerous and illegal. You made it sound like we would be interfering with God and country if we made one wrong move. Damn it, Rafe! We were only planning to do what you were already doing!"

Rafe reached out, snagged her arm and brought her to a halt in front of him. He placed a finger on her soft lips, stopping her flow of muttered comments, and looked down into indignant, hazel eyes. She simmered, fairly radiating passion. He had seen it in one form or another since their first meeting: in his office, in the parlor with her family and just now as she stomped around in irritation. He knew with absolute certainty that the next place he wanted to see it was in his bed.

"I didn't lie to you," he said, leaning back onto the wooden rail and drawing her closer.

Dani stiffened in resistance. Damn those dark eyes! The man was an absolute menace. Elise should never have turned him loose on a world of unsuspecting women. "Maybe you didn't lie," she said stoutly, "but you certainly *implied*."

With a slight tug Rafe edged her between his knees. "Everything I said was true," he insisted.

"There's truth, and then there's *truth*," she pointed out vaguely to his striped tie, wondering how she had ended up with her chin resting against his chest. Just a second ago she had been resisting the pull of his warm, strong hand, she reflected hazily, and now he had his arms wrapped around her, holding her so close she could feel the blast of heat from his body and the steady beat of his heart through the sexy silk shirt.

Rafe tucked a bent finger under her chin and gently lifted. Dani resisted until it became obvious that she was in the midst of a no-win situation. Blinking at the perfectly tied knot of his tie, she considered the fact that Rafe was bulldog tenacious, and far more patient and muscular than she. This, she decided, was

clearly not the time for a display of stubbornness.
Trying to ignore her thudding pulse, she glanced up.

It wasn't easy to meet such a possessive gaze with
even a semblance of equanimity, Dani informed herself. She had, since the magic of adolescence, rear-
ranged her thin body into one of intriguing hollows
and curves, received a flattering number of interested
masculine glances, both surreptitious and overt. It
was, she had decided somewhere along the way, both
gratifying and good for the ego. However, she had
never run into the likes of Rafe Sutherland's gambler's gaze. It said straight out that he wanted her and
intended to have her.

Interesting as it might be to take him on, she
thought with a tug of regret, now was not the time to
add more to her plate. Pulling Jim out of the soup was
about all she could handle at the present. Although,
she hedged, taking a quick peek at the hard face above
her, the challenge was almost irresistible. Apparently
Rafe had never learned that wanting didn't automatically mean getting. It was time he did.

Rafe's bland expression should have been reassuring, she thought idly. But something about his absolute stillness made her think of a hunter patiently
waiting for his prey to fall into a trap. She lowered her
lashes thoughtfully and decided that for once in her
life she should think ahead. If ever there had been a
time to move cautiously, this was it.

Think, Dani warned herself, feeling Rafe's arms
tighten fractionally. It wasn't all that easy, with his
clean, subtly spicy scent invading her every pore, but
this time, she resolved, she was going to deal with a
problem logically. Logic, she reminded herself, was
Arthur's panacea for most of the problems in the

world. Another one, one of his favorite dicta, was the one about never overextending yourself. Naturally he was referring to finances, but she had occasionally found that his axiom applied equally well in other areas of her life.

She had to admit that she wasn't exactly the world's best at recognizing her own limitations. She was the eternal optimist, believing that she could accomplish whatever she chose to do. That, she had learned after several unfortunate experiences, was not always true. Therefore, she rationalized, in this case, moving cautiously might be to her advantage. She was getting the definite feeling that taking on Rafe Sutherland would be a case of biting off far more than she could chew. No, she decided reluctantly after a final glance upward, she'd better leave the teaching of lessons to someone with more time and experience.

Her decisive tone expressed her new resolution. "Rafe, I think we should talk—"

"Later." He lowered his head, his lips lightly brushing hers.

The curiosity Dani had been feeling flared into anticipation. When his mouth touched hers again, she parted her lips.

Rafe's kiss was aggressive, he made no effort to conceal his hunger. Dani's hands on his shoulders tightened, and Rafe told himself that he would let her go if she resisted. If he could. Then, relieved that the decision did not have to be made, his taut muscles eased fractionally as her hands slid around his neck.

Fabric rustled as Rafe's hands traced the inward, utterly feminine curve from hip to waist and hesitated momentarily at breasts that seemed designed expressly to fill his palms. At her sudden indrawn breath they slid upward, fingers touching the slim straps of her sundress, coming to rest only when they framed her face. The silence on the dark porch was broken by a soft sound, somewhere between a whisper and a moan, coming from the back of her throat.

That's right, Rafe thought exultantly, his blood surging heavily through his veins, sing for me. Tell me...

The sound of the screen door opening put an end to both his thoughts and the kiss. Zak flipped on the porch lights and swung over to them, a hideous scowl distorting his face.

"Hell." Rafe closed his eyes and sighed in disgust. "Are you always chaperoned by him?" he demanded, opening his eyes again to examine her face.

Dani glanced over his shoulder, not quite ready to meet his gaze. That had not been a typical first kiss. Nor was it the usual preliminary to artful seduction. What it had been was a clear-cut declaration of intent!

Zak tugged her toward the door, and she followed willingly, Rafe right at her heels. Before he could do more than mutter that he'd be back the next day, Elise's clear voice carried into the hall.

"What should I wear?"

"I've always found black appropriate," Nicholas said.

His tone of understated satisfaction alerted Dani. Unfortunately Rafe did not have that advantage. When they appeared in the doorway Elise looked up, her dark eyes sparking with excitement.

"Guess what? When Nicholas breaks into Munder's pigsty, I'm going with him!"

Chapter Five

Dani lay on the porch glider, enjoying an unexpected bonus: a free afternoon. Everyone else was gone or occupied. Before Billy Bob left, he had reminded her that she hadn't yet played tourist on any of her visits. He offered to drive her into historic Virginia City. In the face of his enthusiasm it hadn't been easy to turn down a trip to "The Liveliest Ghost Town in the West." But she had. Then she listened politely while he extolled the virtues of Reno and Lake Tahoe, both less than thirty miles away. Again she declined.

Not only did she value her life too much to offer her body as a sacrifice to Billy Bob's hell-bent-for-leather driving, she was tired. She had watched as one member of the family after another took off for parts unknown. Now she had nothing to do except enjoy the solitude and hope that a cool breeze would invade the shady porch. And, if she was lucky, sleep.

She had missed her share of that commodity the night before. Normally she dropped off shortly after her head touched the pillow, but last night had been different. The dark hours had passed slowly while kaleidoscopic thoughts of Rafe turned slowly in her mind.

Rafe. In his office that first night. The lazy menace in his eyes when, from her position on the floor, she slowly raised her face and gazed up at him. Rafe in the parlor, meeting her family. His neutral, courteous expression changing first to baffled disbelief, then resolution. The aura of masculinity that had emanated from him. His comfort with it, his casual acceptance of it. And her reaction to it.

Stunned was a fair description, she decided, nodding analytically. She hadn't expected him to radiate such danger signals. Signals that, defying intellect and common sense, beckoned her closer, close enough to his fire to be burned. Taken individually, his obvious physical strength, wit, sense of control, to name only a few potent qualities, did not seem hazardous. Collectively, they were lethal.

It wasn't fair, she thought in mild complaint. Women shouldn't be expected to cope with a man like that. On a scale of one to ten, he leveled out at approximately fourteen. And she didn't have the experience to handle someone like that. Moving her hips just enough to start the swing swaying, she settled back with a sigh, brooding about life's injustices. Having to confront a man like Rafe was bad enough without losing a night's sleep.

The grumbling thought merely served to complete the circle. Rafe. In the kitchen. His wicked grin as she attempted to garnish his elegant dessert. His intent expression as he probed into her past, trying to figure out what made her tick. And Rafe on the porch. Last night. The waiting look in his eyes, serving notice that, while he was patient, there were limits. And when he had touched her, she would have sworn that the floorboards of the porch had trembled. All in all, she thought, it had been a bit like a Southern Californian's first experience with an earthquake. Nothing to hold on to, nothing solid amid the upheaval. Unlike enduring a quake, however, in Rafe she had found something substantial.

Deliberately moving away from that dangerous area, she smiled reminiscently as she pictured the look on his face when Elise had delivered her bombshell. He'd hustled his mother out of the house so fast she barely had time to say goodbye. If this were the Victorian era, Dani decided drowsily, he would be forcibly confining her to the house, or preparing to send her on an extended cruise. All to keep her away from Nicholas. Interesting.

The combination of warmth and the scent of pine-laden air eventually lulled her to sleep. She didn't hear the sound of a car door closing, or footsteps on the wooden stairs. She didn't see Rafe come to a sudden halt, lean against the porch rail and gaze down at her. And, most of all, she missed adding another picture to her mental collection of Rafe's expressions: one of pure, undisguised hunger.

After a few minutes the bright afternoon sunlight beating down on his back grew uncomfortably warm. He rose, snagged a padded chair and, moving with the silence of a shadow, settled close to the swing. With an effort he forced his body to relax.

Dani slept with the total relaxation of a child, one hand close to her cheek, her fingers softly curved. Rafe's dark eyes narrowed, watching as a small smile lifted the corners of her mouth. He'd give a lot to know what she was dreaming about, he thought, resisting the temptation to touch the soft fullness of her lower lip. He leaned back, never taking his eyes off her face. Without the lurking humor in her eyes and the lively intelligence that normally animated her face, it was almost like watching another woman. No less attractive, he decided, giving in to the impulse to brush his thumb along her delicate jaw, just different.

Dani yawned, tensed her body in a luxurious stretch and slowly opened her eyes. The first thing she saw was a pair of gleaming brown boots, crossed and propped on a chair next to the glider. Shifting her eyes, she followed a pair of neatly creased jeans covering long masculine legs to another chair. Sternly disciplining an excited thump in the region of her chest, she examined a brown leather belt. There were no studs or gaudy ornamentation on it, she noted without surprise. It was, like everything else the man wore, simple and elegant. The sleeves of his creamy shirt were rolled up a couple of times, exposing tanned forearms covered with crisp dark hair. His cowboy hat was tugged down over his forehead, almost concealing his eyes. But not quite. There was a speculative gleam in them that Dani didn't trust. He also looked too complacent. She was tempted to reach up and tug on his sexy mustache, but, after another quick glance at his eyes, resisted the impulse.

"Hi," she said cautiously.

He nodded, a half smile tilting one side of his mustache.

"Been here long?"

He nodded again, this time a bit judiciously. "Long enough."

Dani narrowed her eyes in suspicion. "Long enough for what?"

Rafe grinned. "To find out how you'd look in bed."

Knowing she was going to hate herself for doing it, Dani took the bait. Swinging her feet to the floor, she said with a snap, "And how is that?"

He deliberately waited long enough for her temper to flare before he spoke. "Delicious."

"Oh," Dani said, taken aback. No one had ever called her delicious before. She tried the word on for size and decided it wasn't half bad. In fact, not bad at all. "Thank you," she finally added politely.

"You're welcome."

The courteous words matched his tone and tossed the conversational hot potato back to her. Where does one go after one has been told she's delicious? Dani wondered blankly. After a baleful glance at her lounging companion she decided that, wherever it was, he wasn't going to help her get there.

"I thought you'd be busy counting last night's winnings," she said uneasily, wishing he would say something.

He tugged his hat farther down on his forehead. "That's what I have an accountant for."

"Don't you have to check your liquor supply?"

"My bartender does that."

"Change your locks so no more burglars get in?"

"Security," he said succinctly.

"Well what do *you* do?" Besides walking around in a tailor-made tux, dazzling every woman in the place, she added silently. Smoothing the pleats on her shorts, she waited.

He aimed a lazy half smile at her. "Delegate."

Her answering flash of teeth informed him that she didn't believe it. He probably worked longer and harder than any member of his staff. He wasn't the absentee landlord type. Dani sat up straighter, her narrow gaze sharpening in suspicion. "Why do I have the feeling that you came out here with some of that delegating in mind? You want me to do something, don't you?"

The part of his face visible beneath his hat was covered with injured innocence. Even his mustache looked misunderstood.

Slumping against the back of the swing, she said flatly, "It's not going to work. I'm not going to do one thing for the rest of the day. I'm not going to burn one calorie. I may not even move off this swing."

With the tip of one finger Rafe shoved his hat back an inch or two. His dark eyes queried her amiably.

"Don't look at me with that puppy dog expression," she ordered, telling herself that she wouldn't smile. "I'm on vacation. The only energy I plan to expend in the next two weeks is whatever it takes to get Jim's contract back. Other than that—nothing. Zip."

Rafe extended his hand and placed it on her thigh. His eyes gleamed at her expression. She was watching his hand as if it were a snake. His voice brought her head up. "How about doing nothing in my pool?" Before she could shake her head, he added, "You can float all afternoon. Don't have to swim a stroke."

Dani was tempted. If she was smart, she warned herself, she'd stay as far away from him as she could. He would offer her nothing on a long-term basis, and she had never been big on dead-end situations. She was not about to become a gambler's lady, not on any terms.

"The water's nice," he enticed. "And it's going to get hot this afternoon."

"It's already hot."

"Hotter," he amended.

"How do you know?" she asked doubtfully.

Rafe looked up at the cloudless sky. "This time of year, it always gets hotter."

Dani weighed the lure of a pool against the undeniable fact that she was playing with fire. Being around Rafe was as risky as setting a match to the Southern California hills in the dry season. One spark was all it took. And she had the feeling that Rafe, like the weather, would only get hotter.

In a matter of seconds she made up her mind, and logic had nothing to do with her decision. In less than ten minutes she had collected her bathing suit, secured the house and waited while Rafe opened the car door for her.

He slid into his seat, the motion an unconscious blending of hard muscle and smooth coordination. Turning the key in the ignition, he glanced down at her. "Ready?"

She nodded, refusing to read anything into the question other than the obvious. "Ready."

Once the car had traversed the curving drive and turned onto the main road with a barely restrained aggressiveness that reminded her of its owner, she gave in to curiosity and asked, "Where do you live?"

"On the edge of town."

"Carson City?"

He nodded. "Um-hmm."

"Not at the casino?"

He slanted an interested glance at her wary face. Her tone implied that the site was no better than a den of iniquity and that he probably never left the place. He wondered exactly what sort of life-style her vivid imagination had conjured up for him. "I have a small apartment there," he said noncommittally.

"Oh." It probably came with a revolving door and a procession of beautiful women. Finding the idea unreasonably irritating, she scowled at some rust-colored cows complacently grazing behind a barbed wire fence.

"If I'd known you hated cattle so much I'd have gone another way," Rafe commented.

"What?" Dani looked first at his bland expression, then out across the broad stretch of valley, dotted with a lot more cows of various colors. "They don't bother me," she said in surprise. "As long as they're on one side of the fence and I'm on the other." After another glance, encompassing both sides of the road, she added, "That's a lot of milk out there."

Rafe winced, taking his eyes off the road and staring at her in disbelief. She was serious, he realized. She probably thought someone came out with a milk stool and pail and tended them twice a day.

"Beef," he said succinctly. "You're looking at meat on the hoof. This isn't a dairy farm."

"Sorry," she said, raising her brows. "I'm a city girl, remember? As far as I'm concerned, a cow's a cow."

"Unless it's a steer or a bull," he informed her.

"Right," she agreed, her vague tone informing him that she couldn't care less.

"Do you mind making a stop at the casino before we go to the house?" he asked, abruptly changing the subject. "It's not open, but there's something I want to do."

She shook her head. "Fine with me. Can I go in and browse around?"

His mustache twitched. "Want to see the front part this time?"

"It'll be a nice change," she agreed serenely.

He pulled into an underground parking space with his name on it and walked around to open her door. He led her over to a gleaming wood-framed doorway, withdrew a small key from his pocket and inserted it into a gleaming brass lock. A thick door slid to one side.

"Private elevator?" Dani murmured. "I'm impressed."

He shrugged. "Just one of the perks of being the boss."

They got out on the first floor, and Rafe looked directly up at a small camera, nodding in acknowledgement.

"Is there someone here?" Dani asked in surprise.

"Security," he said laconically. "Twenty-four hours a day." He dropped his hand to the small of her back. "The main casino is here," he said. He flipped switches that flooded the room with light, and stopped, examining her stunned expression.

The room was beautiful, striking without the garishness so prevalent in many such establishments. A deeply piled jonquil carpet, in stunning contrast to the green baize-covered tabletops, extended a silent invitation. Crystal chandeliers added their own brand of elegance to the room. All it needed was patrons clad in formal evening clothes to bring it to life.

Dani nodded, impressed. She walked down the ebony steps, stopping at a baccarat table. There were no slot machines, she noted with approval. The raucous clatter of coins would have been an intrusion in the exquisitely tasteful room. She looked back over her shoulder to the silent man watching her so intently. "A real class act, Rafe," she lauded. "*I'd* even be tempted to try my luck here."

"Repeat that when my mother's around and you'll have a friend for life."

Dani's brows arched inquiringly. "Why?"

His gaze took in the entire room. "Because she handled the interior design."

Pursing her lips in a soundless whistle of appreciation, Dani said, "I wonder if she'd consider going back to L.A. with me. My condo could use her talent." Ignoring his sudden frown, she said quickly, "Speaking of your mother, I enjoyed meeting her last night. She's a charming lady."

"Yes, she is," he agreed. "She's also in excellent health, and that's the way I want to keep her."

"I beg your pardon?" she said blankly.

"I don't want her getting mixed up with your family and their crazy schemes. I especially don't want her getting carried away with—"

"Nicholas?" she interrupted in a cool voice that concealed a sudden, hot surge of anger.

His long legs covered the distance between them. "Right the first time." He applauded. "That's exactly who I mean."

"Look here, Rafe Sutherland," she began, prodding his chest with a slim finger, abandoning all pretense of composure. "*I'm* not the one who couldn't keep his mouth shut over dinner. *I'm* not the one who drove her out to the house. *I'm* not—"

"Oh, hell," he said in disgust, raking his fingers through his thick hair and looking down at her. She was sixty-five inches of pure outrage, a she-bear protecting her cubs. "Look, honey—"

"Don't 'honey' me," she said fiercely. "The name is Danita."

"All I'm trying to say is—"

"That you don't want your mother to have anything to do with us. Right?"

"Right!" As her eyes narrowed in increasing fury, he swore. "Damn it, Dani, I don't mean that, and you know it. I just don't want her breaking her neck, or getting shot by one of Munder's goons. Is that so unreasonable?"

He watched as Dani blinked and the anger drained from her, like shadows dissipating in the morning sunlight. She could understand honest concern. She should, he reflected, remembering what had brought her to Carson City. It seemed that she spent most of her time taking care of other people's problems. And that was another thing he meant to discuss with her. Too many people took advantage of her. But he'd do that later, he decided, scrutinizing the determined tilt of her chin. Much later.

Opening a solid oak door, he gestured for her to precede him.

"What am I supposed to do if she comes to the house?" Dani asked, gnawing at the conversation like a bone. "Lock the door? Tell her she can't come in? I can't do that," she argued, following him up a flight of stairs. "And I can't do anything about Nicholas. Nicholas is a law unto himself."

She stopped midway and contemplated his back. "Your mother looks like a, uh, resolute sort of woman and—"

"'Stubborn' is the word you're looking for," he interrupted, not even slowing down.

"Determined," she compromised.

"Mulish."

"Whatever. Anyway, I'm not about to get between her and whatever she wants." Especially if it's Nicholas, she thought. "No," she continued, "I'm not your mother's keeper. If you want her incommunicado, you're the one who'll have to rip out the phones and chain her to the wall."

He stopped, turning to look down at her. "You do have a tendency to get dramatic, don't you?"

"Am I right?" she demanded, the green-gold of her eyes intent on him.

Sighing sharply, he nodded. "You're right."

Her good humor restored by his admission, Dani's lips curved in a slight smile. "I'm surprised you let her out of your sight today."

"I had no choice. Nicholas came by to pick her up."

"Really?"

"Your mouth's open," he informed her. "Yes, really."

Dani closed her mouth and absentmindedly climbed the rest of the stairs. "I wonder what they're up to?" she said slowly.

Rafe withdrew another key from his pocket and inserted it into another brass lock. "Probably buying her some crepe-soled shoes and a basic black, breaking and entering outfit." Without waiting for her reaction, he turned the key, then opened the door and held it for her.

Mulling over the ramifications of his last statement, she automatically stepped forward—into a world far removed from the elegant decor downstairs. Her gaze flicked over a utilitarian desk-and-worktable that ran the length of the room and settled on a bank of television monitors covering the far wall.

Rafe touched her elbow, gently nudging her forward. After introducing her to the two men working at the table and keeping an eagle eye on the monitors, he nodded at the wall and said, "This is what I wanted to show you."

Dani walked closer, fascinated, as the images on the screen flicked from one location to another.

"Look familiar?" Rafe asked, pointing to one.

She nodded. It was the back entrance and hallway she had used the night Rafe discovered her rummaging through his files.

"Watch," he directed, tapping a button. The hall faded in a blink, replaced by the solid oak door of his office.

After a moment's observation she winced, realizing just how easily they had followed her movements that night. In contrast, she thought, watching the other monitors, the entry Nicholas had effected was just short of miraculous. No, not that, she decided after a moment's reflection. It was pure skill. He had done his homework. He had also gone in the right door. Luck had nothing at all to do with it.

"I suppose this was set up scientifically," she commented. "With all the angles covered."

"I thought so," Rafe said, frowning thoughtfully at the screens. "But if Nicholas really got in here the night before you did, we've got a problem."

"He really did."

"Damn."

"You know," she said slowly, "if you asked him, he'd come down and do it again."

"Terrific. All I need is a burglar running loose in the place."

She shook her head. "No, really. He does it all the time."

"I know," Rafe said in a dry voice, "you told me."

"I told you what he used to do, and how he occasionally does something for kicks. But that's only part of it. I didn't tell you what he does *professionally*."

Rafe sighed. "What?"

Grinning, Dani said, "He breaks into places *legally*."

"I'm sorry I asked."

"I'm serious," she said, tugging at his sleeve as he turned away. When she had his complete attention she continued. "Nicholas works for one of the best security companies in the country. After they install their system he goes in looking for bugs. When he finds them, he tells the people how to beef up the security."

"My God." The amused fascination in his tone brought her eyes up to meet his.

"He'd do it for you," she promised blithely. "He does it for all his friends. He dropped in on Brady six or seven times. That was before Brady married my mother."

"I bet he loved that," Rafe commented.

"Brady didn't mind, but his security firm got pretty annoyed. Actually, Brady got off pretty cheap. It only cost him a glass of his best brandy each time Nicholas found a new way in."

"I think I'll pass."

"You don't have to say anything to him," she assured Rafe.

"Good."

"I'll do it."

Rafe dropped his arm lightly around her shoulders and turned her to face him. "Dani, listen to me," he began, but he drew to a halt when she placed her finger over his lips.

"Actually, you'd be doing Nicholas a favor. He's in between jobs right now, and if he doesn't have something to do there's no telling what sort of mischief he'll get into." *And drag your mother along with him,* she added mentally.

Mischief. Spelled trouble. Such as breaking into Jed Munder's place, Rafe thought. And involving my mother in the mess. Looking at it that way, it might not be a bad idea to keep Nicholas occupied. "I'll think about it," he promised.

"Good." Dani nodded in satisfaction. "When will you ask him?"

Rafe gave an exasperated sigh. "In a day or so. Okay?"

"Very," she said with a smile. Turning away, she asked, "What else do you have in here to foil the local bad guys?"

"Several convenient little gadgets, but they're not important. What *is* important is that—"

"I think I hear the beginning of a lecture," Dani muttered audibly.

"You see the kind of technology that's available. And you can bet your sweet little butt that if I have something—"

"I *knew* it. A lecture."

"Munder has a bigger one and more of it. I just want you to understand how crazy it is to even consider breaking into his place."

"Rafe," she said patiently, "I know you think I'm impulsive and irresponsible, and I really can't blame you. That fiasco in your office wasn't exactly the kind of thing that would inspire confidence. I admit that even if the worst happens and your plan doesn't work, I'm not experienced enough to tackle his place."

Rafe let out a long sigh, surprised at the degree of relief he felt at hearing her words.

"But Nicholas is. And this time I'd follow his instructions to the letter."

Dark eyes narrowed in pure exasperation. Rafe's mustache twitched as he uttered a succinct, sibilant oath.

"You don't realize it yet," Dani said, heading for the door, "but Nicholas is an artist, an absolute genius."

"I don't give a damn if he's Salvador Dali," he snarled, almost treading on her heels as he followed her down the stairs. "I don't want you anywhere near him when he does one of his midnight flits."

She walked through the outer door and waited while he unlocked the car. "You really don't have anything to say about it," she reminded him quietly.

There was a definite pause before he spoke. A heavy, dark, dangerous pause. Inclining his head politely, he opened the door. "As you say."

Dani allowed herself to be stuffed into the car, wondering why those three little words set her teeth on edge. Probably, she told herself, because she didn't believe one syllable of them. Somewhere along the way Rafe had, as he so colorfully expressed it, dealt himself in, and she didn't see him giving up until he won the entire pot.

He slid behind the steering wheel and looked down with a smile that was pure challenge. "Now how about that swim?"

Chapter Six

He was watching her. She didn't need to open her eyes to be certain. She could feel it.

The cool water lapped gently around her. Leaves of a nearby oak, stirred by a soft breeze, blocked the slanting rays of the afternoon sun. Shadows touched her face, momentarily dimming the light against her eyelids.

"Your nose is getting red." Rafe's voice was closer than she'd expected and she squinted, opening one eye. He was standing at the edge of the pool just a few feet away.

Dani opened her other eye and stared. He was worth the effort. Dark, springy hair covered his chest, dipped into his brief bathing suit and ran down long, muscular legs. She swallowed and lifted her hand to touch a cool finger to her warm nose. "I suppose I could turn over," she said lazily, deliberately closing her eyes again to banish the tempting, masculine image.

"You could try," he agreed in a carefully amiable voice.

Almost everything about him had been circumspect and benign for the past couple of hours. It was as if, now that she was on his turf, he had decided to step back from his pointed challenge. Earlier that afternoon he had driven past a discreet sign that said *Sutherlands*, brought her to his house, led her into the backyard and pointed to the dressing room. When she emerged, he was swimming. She had slid into the pool and done nothing more strenuous than float on her back, watching him through slitted eyes as he surged through the water doing lap after lap. He swam as he did everything else, without apparent effort. Then he'd hauled himself out of the deep end with a smooth rush, settled on a chaise and directed an occasional comment to her.

He had his voice on a tight leash. And that, in itself, was suspicious. She could count on the fingers of one hand—and still have a couple left over—the times he had been this casual. He was usually hell-bent on ordering her around or knocking her off her feet with his own brand of potent, masculine charm. Now he was doing neither. At least, not yet.

His restraint was remarkable, she thought warily, wondering how long it would last. There wasn't a thing about him that wasn't controlled—except his eyes. And, if her instincts were running true to form, he hadn't taken them off her since he'd left the pool.

His deep voice interrupted her uneasy train of thought. "How about something cool to drink?"

"Sounds great," she said, without opening her eyes. "Can you pipe it down to me?"

"I might be able to arrange it, but if you don't want your face as red as a mountain sunset, you'd better get in the shade."

"That bad?" she asked, reluctantly opening one eye.

He nodded. "Getting there. This way," he added as she turned over and swam smoothly toward the side.

"I can't get out without a ladder," she complained mildly, stopping to tread water.

Rafe looked down at her as she blinked iridescent beads of water from her lashes. She had no makeup on, her honey brown hair was woven into a fat braid, she looked far too young to induce the thoughts that were possessing him and in about thirty seconds she was going to know exactly what effect she was having on his body. "I'll help," he said evenly. "Give me your hands."

With a minimum of fuss he tugged her smoothly out of the water and lowered her slowly until her feet touched the deck. A soft sound lodged in Dani's throat as her water-cooled body brushed down the length of his. She stepped back and moved away, a bit too quickly. So much for nonchalance, she thought wryly.

The shaded patio was cooler, a distinct relief from the heat of blazing sunshine and masculinity. Rafe indicated a large, fatly padded double chaise. After one quick, dubious glance at him, she sat, swung up her feet and reached for the tall glass of fruit juice that he handed her.

She could almost feel him turn off his sensuality. It was as physical and distinct as when he had released her hands. Now, apparently satisfied with the jolt he had given her, he stretched out beside her on the chaise and leaned back with closed eyes. That was fine with her, she decided. She wasn't ready to cope with his potent brand of charm and challenge. Especially not when she had so many other things requiring her attention. And God only knew there were plenty of them. Things were getting entirely out of hand at home. She was going to have to do something. The question was, what?

Several minutes later, Rafe opened his eyes and examined her contemplative expression with increasing distrust. She was trying to cover her abstraction with a look of utter innocence—and failing miserably.

"It's a good thing you don't gamble," he said abruptly.

She looked up at him and blinked. Her gaze sharpened to green-and-gold inquiry. "Why?"

"You don't exactly have a poker face," he pointed out.

Sighing in exaggerated exasperation, Dani asked, "Do you think I could cultivate an enigmatic one?"

"I wouldn't bet on it."

"I don't bet on anything," she reminded him.

Propping himself on the elbow nearest her, he said, "Believe me, that's to your advantage."

Dani tilted her glass and swallowed with polite greed, averting her gaze from his broad shoulders, which loomed over her more than a tad too close.

"What kind of plot are you hatching now?" he demanded, his eyes narrowed on her face.

"What I'm doing," she said calmly, looking out at the lush expanse of grass beyond the pool, "is called relaxing. Nothing more, nothing less." She propped her outsize sunglasses on her nose and hid behind them.

Rafe made a rude noise. "You're up to your eye-balls in plots, and they all have to do with Munder."

"No plots," she soothed, wishing he didn't look quite so grim. "Just a few random thoughts. Considering options, that sort of thing."

"You gave me three days," he stated, staring down at his reflection in the gray-tinted glasses.

"That's right, and your time is up at midnight," she reminded him calmly. "Tonight."

"And you can't wait to put your neck on the line, can you?"

Dani sat up with a jerk. "Do you think I *like* doing crazy stuff like this?" she demanded. Not waiting for an answer, she said firmly, "I don't. I haven't got nerves of steel like Nicholas. The only reason I even attempted your office was because Nicholas took me through every step of the plan. And—" she eyed him stonily, daring him to make even one comment "—I'd have been all right if I had followed directions."

Rafe's lips parted. Before he could utter a sound, Dani held up her hand, palm toward him. "I hope your plans work. I hope your man comes out with everything you need to break Jed Munder. But if he doesn't," she assured him softly, "as sure as God made little green apples, Nicholas and I will be going in there."

With a sharp sigh Rafe dropped back onto the chaise. He hoped to God that tonight would be the end of this whole mess. If not, he'd have to hog-tie her to keep her away from the Golden Boar. And he'd do it if he had to. Otherwise she'd mess around and eventually get herself killed by Munder. And if Munder didn't do it, he thought grimly, he might just tackle the job himself.

"What are the rest of them up to?" he asked, almost hoping that she wouldn't tell him.

"Don't ask," she advised dryly. "You know I have this compulsion to tell the truth, and believe me, you don't want to hear it."

"Talk," he said. "I'll bear up somehow." He held up one finger. "Nicholas first."

"He's studying the blueprints of the Golden Boar."

Rafe's head swiveled sideways and he stared at her composed profile. "The what?"

Dani waved a hand as if the air would miraculously produce an explanation. "You know, architectural drawings, things like that." She slid her glasses up until they perched on top of her head. "Rafe, I can't begin to tell you the pile of papers he has. He's got roof plans, elevation views—whatever they are—site plans and ladder diagrams. They're the ones that show the smoke and fire alarms," she added kindly as a frown pulled his brows together.

He drew in a deep breath. "I know what they are. I have the ones for my place. Will you tell me how in the hell," he asked repressively, "he managed to get those drawings?"

"Connections," she said succinctly. "I never ask—he never tells."

Rafe scowled and held up a second finger. "Arthur."

Dani's smile was one of amused affection. "He's reading articles on hackers, trying to figure out how to invade Munder's computer system."

A third finger went up. "Billy Bob?"

Her smile grew broader. "He's inviting his high-rolling friends to town for backup or to raise hell just on general principles."

Rafe's little finger moved up to join the others. "Emily?"

"Emily," she said, "is having a benefit for her Save the Whale people." She waited, thoroughly enjoying the varied expressions on Rafe's face. They began with consideration, moved to perplexity and stopped somewhere around apprehension.

"Where?" he asked, cutting to the heart of the matter with the single word.

"The Golden Boar." She raised her hand, again halting his words. "You understand we're talking diversionary tactics here," she said, putting her glass on the table and sitting up.

"How did she manage it?"

"She's learned a lot about Munder in the past couple of days. He wants to move up in the world—not in financial terms, in society. He'd give his eyeteeth to rub elbows with your friends and business associates,"

"What's so special about my friends?"

"From where you stand, maybe nothing. But when you're on the outside looking in, a lot. Jed Munder wants to have class. He can't buy it, so now he's trying another approach."

"How? And how did you find out about this?"

"I didn't, Emily did. I don't know how she learns these things, but she's never wrong. If she says it's so, it's so. As to the other how, he's becoming a charitable institution." She waited for a comment, but for once Rafe seemed struck dumb. "He's turning one of his rooms into a banquet hall to be used for philanthropic purposes. He's calling it the Jed Munder Room and it will be available free of charge to any service organization or charity. Emily's got an appointment with him tomorrow and she's going to set a date for late next week. Whatever date they select will launch his entire program.''

"And what if everything is settled tonight?"

"Then she'll call him tomorrow and explain that the benefit has to be delayed because her group has to chase down a Russian trawler that's killing whales." She leaned back, enormously entertained by his look of morose fascination.

His thumb joined the four fingers. "Tabitha?"

Dani grinned. "Munder needs publicity when he launches the Jed Munder Room. Emily got the room on such short notice because Tabitha promised to bring Zak and maybe a few other celebrities for the occasion."

Rafe rubbed his finger between his tightly knit brows. "My God."

"It sounds just like them, doesn't it? But they have such a wonderful time planning these things, I don't have the heart to stop them," Dani said, a smile lifting the corners of her mouth.

"And you will be with Nicholas." It was more statement than question.

"I don't know," she said vaguely, her eyes hazy with thought. "I thought of something today that has definite possibilities." Before he could ask any more questions, she changed the subject quickly. "But if we're lucky, it'll all be settled tonight."

"If we're not, tell me when the big day is so I can lock up my mother."

The trouble with Rafe was that he didn't know whether to believe her or not, Dani reflected. Finding her in his office should have made a believer out of him, and possibly it did where she was concerned. But he had never seen the rest of them in action. He didn't know if they would actually stir themselves or if they were all talk. And for now perhaps that was best. If his plans didn't work out, he would know soon enough.

"Does Elise live here?"

Rafe's gaze settled on her face. The question was not as inconsequential as it sounded. It was definitely a change of subject. If he wanted to discuss families, he would now discuss his own.

He shook his head. "No, she's still in the family house. It's a few miles back toward town."

Dani looked up at the rambling roofline of the white, woodframed house. "It's nice," she said with vast understatement. "How long have you been here?"

"Almost five years."

Her eyes moved to his in surprise. She estimated that he was no more than five or six years older than her own twenty-five years. He had been young to buy a property this large. Unless she was mistaken about his age. He could be—

"Thirty-two," he said, reading her thoughts as easily as if they had been typed on her forehead.

"That could get to be annoying," she said equably. "Why this particular house?"

He slanted a look down at her. "Why not? Don't you like it?"

"I love it," she said promptly. "I'm just surprised that you bought such a big place."

"I like a lot of room." He lifted the insulated pitcher on the table beside him and leaned over to fill her glass. "Besides, it came with a few acres that I wanted."

Dani sucked in her breath, hardly hearing his answer. His arm brushed her breasts as he leaned across her. It wasn't intentional. It didn't matter. Her body responded as if he had deliberately stroked her to arousal. Even then, she might have gotten away with it if she hadn't automatically stiffened.

He glanced down, his eyes skimming over her face and instinctively settling on her bikini top. Without moving his gaze, he carefully set the carafe next to her glass. Dani's eyes shifted from his intent expression to the jade-green material of her suit. The damp fabric faithfully shaped itself to the changing contours of her breasts, clinging to the betraying beads of her nipples.

Rafe removed his arm, meticulously avoiding contact with her body. He leaned on one elbow, his chest and shoulders hovering over her, while a glimmer of a smile curved his lips and tilted his mustache. "Well, hello," he said softly. "Welcome to Sutherlands."

Dani glared up at him. If she had had any chance at all of gaining control of the situation, it had just been lost. And all it had taken was the sound of his voice. The words had been bad enough, but the voice was the killer. It evoked images of raindrops on parched skin, a banquet for the hungry and promises for a woman who hadn't known she wanted a man.

"Now look," she said valiantly, "this doesn't mean a thing."

"I know," he soothed, brushing a finger over the satiny skin just above the edge of her suit, watching with interest as a tremor shook her body. "It probably happens all the time."

"Not exactly," she muttered. Not even close.

Lowering his head slowly, giving her time to object, he touched his lips to the pulse in her neck, his mustache brushing softly against her collarbone. "I need to know something," he said, satisfaction warming his voice when she shivered again.

"What?" Stop him, she told herself. Now. Before it's too late. Before he does a number on you with that sexy mustache. "Rafe—"

"Is there a man in your life?" he asked, touching his lips to her shoulder.

"Man?" she asked vaguely, ignoring the brisk, commonsense voice within.

"As in lover? Significant other? Fiancé? Whatever."

Even as she gave a slow shake of her head in response to each question, Dani was snared by his demanding gaze. His eyes, so deep a brown they seemed black, were actually alive with tiny prisms of light. They held hers, questioning, reading, and finally freeing her with a blink of dark lashes.

"Ah."

"What does that mean? Ah, as in 'she's ripe for the plucking'?" she asked, belatedly listening to the agitated voice within her.

"No. More along the line of 'she's a beautiful desirable woman and she's not sharing her bed with a man.'"

"She shares her bed as infrequently as she gambles," Dani informed him dryly, planting a finger in the mat of hair on his chest and prodding. When he didn't move, she exerted a little more force. When that had no effect, she sighed sharply and said, "Rafe, this is—"

"If you're about to give me the this-is-so-sudden routine, I just may have to do something drastic here." One hand smoothed her braid across her slender neck.

"Threats will get you nowhere," she said, more relieved than she would have believed at his whimsical tone. "Besides, it *is* too sudden."

"Too soon to get you in my bed?"

"Absolutely."

"Too soon to discuss the possibility of a serious relationship?"

As in an affair? she wondered. "Definitely."

"Too soon for a kiss?"

Now *there* was a question. A double-edged sword if ever there was one. Since they'd already entered that territory the night before, a yes would be ridiculous. And a no would be an open invitation.

"I thought not," he murmured.

His face came closer, till all Dani could focus on was his eyes. His gorgeous eyes with pinpoints of wicked light, beckoning, enticing, tantalizing.

Except for the cushion beneath her, she was surrounded by nothing but Rafe. The long warmth of his body lay along one side; his wrist brushed her waist on the other. One forearm was braced above her head; his foot nudged the bottom of hers, and his shoulders hovered over her, diminishing her area of vision to a broad chest covered with crisp, dark hair.

His lips touched, slanting across hers in a possessive action that left her stomach fluttering and her lungs in desperate need of air. The man didn't seem to have a brotherly or avuncular kiss in his repertoire, she thought dimly. His expertise was undeniable—obviously he didn't spend *all* his time behind gaming ta-

bles—and the results leaned heavily toward the "Me,
Tarzan, you, Jane" variety.

Dani's hands settled on his shoulders. She intended
to apply a little force, to get a bit of her own breathing space back. Instead her fingers traced slabs of
muscle, gently kneaded the back of his neck and laced
through his thick, dark hair. Her hands tightened and
she tilted her head, parting her lips, fitting herself to
his touch. The kiss was urgent, hot and endless. When
Rafe broke it off, it was merely to place his mouth on
the racing pulse in her throat. His arm pulled her
closer as she made a soft sound that he felt rather than
heard.

Drawing in a shaky breath Dani considered asking
for her body back. Later, she decided, arching into his
hand as it traced the curve from her rib cage to hip. I'll
definitely do it in a couple of minutes. Two minutes
later her head was resting on his shoulder and her body
was held against his, responding to the tantalizing
touch of his hands. Arousal was present and capitu-
lation imminent. For a woman who didn't gamble, she
reflected hazily, she was playing a pretty risky game.

Rafe felt the sudden change, the tentative with-
drawal. "What's the matter?" he murmured against
her temple.

Taking advantage of his fractionally slackened embrace, she edged away until about six inches sepa-
rated them. For the moment, she couldn't think of
anything coherent to say, so she just shook her head.

His eyes narrowing in speculation, he repeated,
"What's the matter?" A rush of pure male satisfaction sharpened his expression as he examined her face.
She apparently wasn't going to satisfy his curiosity,
but she couldn't conceal her heightened color and

rapid pulse. For a brief time, she had been all woman to his man. But judging by her wary look, she had suddenly remembered that he was not on her list of acceptable men.

Dani took a deep breath and exhaled slowly. Now was as good a time as any to set the record straight, she decided. The only time. If she waited, no telling what sort of mess she'd end up in. Averting her gaze from his hard, suddenly expressionless face, she began. "I don't think this is wise, Rafe."

"What isn't?"

She sighed. He wasn't going to make it easy. "This," she said, with a gesture of her hand that included the two of them. "Us. The whole thing. It's asking for nothing but trouble."

"I can handle it."

His abrupt words and hard voice had her shifting edgily. "You probably can," she agreed. "But I can't. If we keep on like this, we're going to end up in bed."

"That's bad?"

She nodded. "That's right. I'm going to be here for twelve more days, then I'm heading back to Los Angeles. I don't plan on having an affair during that time."

"Why not?"

"Because I'm not constitutionally set up for one-night stands and brief affairs. I'm no gambler, Rafe."

"The hell you're not!"

Dani jerked to a sitting position and glared down at him. "What do you mean?"

"Lady, you gamble every day of your life, and the stakes you play for make me look like a piker."

"You're the one who runs a casino!"

"And you're the one who puts her life on the line," he pointed out, dark eyes steady.

"I do not," she protested, avoiding his glance. "You act as if I'm some sort of daredevil, shooting rapids or jumping out of planes."

"Worse than that," he said softly. "You're a woman who cares about people so much you don't count the consequences when you set out to help them."

"You're wrong," she stated, shaking her head. "There's nothing extraordinary about my life. I live quietly and have a regular job. Most of my time is spent behind a desk, for heaven's sake!"

"Except when you're breaking into someone's place of business."

"Oh, that," she said airily, wishing he hadn't so easily found the weak spot in her argument.

"Yeah, that."

"I don't do it all the time," she assured him. "In fact, that was a first."

"You may not want to admit it, may not even believe it, but, Dani, you have the mind-set of a first-class gambler." He ignored her parted lips and indrawn breath. "It's not how often you do something," he persisted, "it's the attitude with which you approach it."

She shook her head in disagreement. "You're wrong," she said flatly.

Rafe leaned back, lacing his fingers behind his head. "What do you call it?" he asked with deep interest.

"Confidence."

"Try again."

"Stupidity?"

"You're a gambler."

And that, apparently, was that. Rafe Sutherland had spoken. The man was maddening. He also had a weird logic that was hard to combat. But in this case, he was wrong. For some reason she was reluctant to pursue, she didn't want him to be right. "Look," she said, resuming the battle with energy, "I think you're overlooking a vital point."

His eyebrows rose questioningly.

"A gambler is aware of the risks involved. He investigates them, evaluates them and then decides whether or not to go forward."

Rafe nodded in encouragement.

"I didn't even think of the danger involved," she said triumphantly. "I just jumped in and did it. That may make me foolhardy, but hardly a risk taker."

"What do you call what you're doing right now?"

"What's that?" she asked cautiously.

"Going ahead with plans to bust Munder's place wide open. I know, you'll only do it if my plan falls apart," he said, raising a hand to stop her protest, "but you'll do it if you have to. Right?"

There was a distinct pause before she said a reluctant, "Right."

"I've pointed out the dangers ad nauseam, right?"

Another pause, another grudging "Right."

"So you know there are risks, right?"

Dani sighed in disgust. "Right."

"And you'll still do it?"

"You're wearing this thing into the ground," she complained. "What's your point?"

"That you, lady, *are* one hell of a gambler!"

Chapter Seven

I'm coming, I'm coming. Just a minute," Dani called, reaching the front hall just as impatient knuckles began another onslaught on the door. She threw it open and absorbed the sight of a grim, slightly rumpled Rafe. Gorgeous, she decided, staring at the formal evening clothes he wore at the casino. Gorgeous, but undeniably rumpled.

"You look like something the cat took a second look at and decided not to drag in," she commented, stepping aside to give him room.

"I feel worse. Got any coffee?"

"You drove all the way out here for a cup of coffee?" she began. Then, taking another look at his face, she decided that questions could wait. She turned on her heel and headed for the kitchen.

He didn't look as if he were any more rested than she felt, Dani decided, reaching for a cup. Pouring the coffee, she thought about yesterday afternoon. She hadn't found his poolside analysis particularly appealing. Things had gone from bad to worse and she'd asked to be brought home before she'd even set foot inside his attractive, rambling house. Of course, she reflected, handing him the steaming cup, his look of exhaustion could just be a result of his life-style. She hadn't figured out exactly when he slept. If he spent his days with her and nights at the casino, it didn't leave a whole lot of time for rest.

So don't start imagining things, she warned herself, watching him swallow the hot brew and pouring a cup for herself. She had lost several hours' sleep pursuing various futile trains of thought. Such as why couldn't he be the owner of a hardware store or something equally innocuous, why couldn't she be the type of woman who would gladly accept him for exactly what he was and, finally, could his psychological profile of her have been right? Even a little bit? The bright light of day had brought no more answers than had the star-studded night.

"Have you had breakfast?"

"What?" Rafe stared into his cup thoughtfully, as if expecting an answer to pop out of it.

Dani waved helpfully toward the stove. "Breakfast? Eggs and stuff?"

"No. I don't think so. I don't remember." Moving his shoulders impatiently, he said, "It doesn't matter."

"Sit," she directed, pointing at a chair by the round oak table. If he didn't have better sense than to skip sleep *and* meals, someone had to do something about it. And apparently she was elected. He sat, scowling impartially at his empty cup and her. She filled the cup, thinking that if he was always this grumpy in the morning, by returning to L.A. she just might be escaping the well-known fate worse than death. Too bad the idea didn't raise her spirits, she reflected, taking some eggs from the refrigerator. Too bad she didn't believe it.

"How do you like them?" she asked.

"Up and unbroken."

Dani turned her back on him, busying herself at the stove and allowing him time to snarl at his coffee in private. Minutes later, she slid a plate before him. He ate with such silent concentration that she wondered if he had also missed dinner the night before. After taking one last bite of toast, he stacked his knife and fork neatly on the plate. Before he could examine his cup again, she filled it.

Rafe looked at the composed woman across from him. He had come to her and she had instinctively supplied coffee, silence, space and food. What he wanted to do now was wrap his arms around her and take her somewhere private, quiet and horizontal. What he had to do was break the bad news.

"Grady ran into trouble," he said bluntly.

Dani's gaze locked with his, suddenly understanding the reason for his bad temper. "Grady?" she asked, hoping she was wrong.

"The man I had working in Munder's place."

"Past tense?"

Rafe gave a grim nod of confirmation. "He got out in one piece just before all hell broke loose. Someone got suspicious and started checking out the more recent employees. His cover was good, but I told him to take off if things got dicey."

"Suspicious of what?" she asked, zeroing in on the word.

"Requests for certain financial records, other information misplaced or missing. Munder's people started mentioning things that taken separately meant nothing, but putting them together made it clear that someone was asking questions they didn't want answered."

"Is he okay?"

Rafe's nod was grim.

"Thank God for that." Dani's voice expressed relief. "Did he get what you needed?"

"No." Rafe moved his saucer meticulously an inch to the right. His precise movement gave her some indication of his massive control. His glance confirmed it. "But before he took off, he gave me everything he had."

"Which was?"

"A lot of rumors and conjecture. Not a shred of solid evidence."

"Damn!"

Dani's mild oath brought a flicker of amusement to his eyes.

"I couldn't agree more." The humor faded as suddenly as it had appeared, settling into lines of grim determination. "I'm going to take great pleasure in nailing Munder's hide to the wall."

She didn't doubt it. But it wouldn't be in time to help her. Or poor Jim. She closed her eyes briefly at the thought. These three days had been a respite, a reprieve. Now it was back to the real world. Both of them knew it; neither of them wanted to say it.

Fiddling with her cup, she asked, "What are you going to do?"

His expression didn't change as he said vaguely, "I've got a plan."

"So do I," she reminded him.

Going on as if she hadn't spoken, he said, "I've been thinking about this for some time. I've needed the right bait, and now I think I have it."

"Bait?"

"Every trap needs it, and something you said yesterday gave me the idea."

Ignoring Dani's sudden look of wide-eyed curiosity, he asked, "Will you trust me for a few more days?"

Her expression altering to one of immense caution, she asked, "Does trusting you mean doing nothing while you implement your plan?"

He nodded, his eyes steady on her face.

Dani resisted the almost overwhelming impulse to grab the dishes from the table, take them to the sink and turn her back on his demanding look. "I'm sorry, Rafe, I can't do that."

"You mean you won't."

She swallowed, wincing at his hard tone. "I guess I do. Look, I know that Jim's problem seems like small potatoes to you, but it isn't to me. I made a promise, and I intend to carry through on it."

"How the hell do you get involved in these crazy things, anyway?" His disgusted tone left her in no doubt of his opinion on the matter.

"I told you," she said defensively. "I don't do stuff like this all the time. But when Jim told me what had happened, all I could think about was Lori and the girls. I grew up with Lori. She's like my own sister. I couldn't let anything happen to her."

"You shouldn't be involved at all," Rafe stated grimly. "Why didn't Jim handle it by himself?"

"He couldn't," Dani said, as if that explained everything. "He's completely out of his element."

"But, why *you*?"

Good question, she thought, wondering how to explain. What made it all the more difficult was that she didn't exactly know why, either. Her friends had always come to her with their problems. And she normally had a solution for them, so, over the years, it had become one of those self-perpetuating things.

"I can usually think of some way to help them," she offered slowly.

"And I suppose you associate with crooks and gamblers all the time."

Dani narrowed her eyes at the pointed sarcasm. "No. You're my first gambler," she pointed out calmly.

And your last, he thought, watching her lazily from beneath lowered lashes. Your one and only. At least, he reflected philosophically, she hadn't grouped him with the crooks.

"So you're going to call in the family and concoct some crazy scheme."

It wasn't a question, she noted. It was more a statement wrapped in resignation. "Nicholas is always careful and thorough. His plan won't be irresponsible."

"No, but the rest of them will be running around doing a routine from a Marx Brothers movie," he said in disgust.

"Rafe, whatever we do, it won't affect you. I know you're looking at this whole thing from another perspective, that your picture is much larger than mine. I want Jim's debt removed from Munder's records. Without it—considering the size of Munder's place and the volume of his business—I don't think he'll even remember it. So our job is to get the paper and destroy the records."

"And what's mine?"

"To change the world," she said, trying to keep her tone light, more disturbed than she wanted to admit by his grim look. "At least, your immediate part of it. The way I understand it is that you want Munder forced out of business in Carson City and out of gambling in general. I haven't the foggiest idea how to bring that about, so I don't think I'd be much help."

"I'm not asking you for solutions." He bit off the words deliberately as he stacked the dishes. "I handle my own problems."

Dani gritted her teeth and smiled, a cool, little curve of lips that did little to conceal her annoyance. "Well, that settles that, doesn't it? You work on your end of it, and I'll take care of mine. That way we won't get in each other's way."

"I could handle yours if you'd give me half a chance." Rafe stepped in front of her, blocking her way to the sink. She ducked around him and turned the water on full force.

"There's no need to worry," she said, raising her voice over the clatter of silverware. "Nicholas will be there."

"Damn it," he said in a muted roar. "*I* want to take care of you. *I* want to be there to pull you out of a tight spot if you need help." Not Nicholas, even if he was old enough to be her grandfather. Not any other man. Only me.

"That's very nice of you," she began carefully. Before she uttered another word, he stopped her.

"I told you once before that 'nice' has nothing to do with it," he said.

Too late, Dani caught the dangerous inflection in his voice. Strong fingers closed around her shoulders, left bare by the bold, yellow halter-neck sundress she wore, and turned her into his arms.

"Rafe!" Her hands lifted, bracing against his shoulders. "This isn't the time to—"

"It's the perfect time," he assured her, lowering his head. His arms tightened, bringing her closer, until the soft warmth of her breasts was crushed against his chest. His lips brushed hers, lingered over the velvety fullness of her lower lip; then his warm mouth came down on hers.

Dani started to struggle, then instinctively stilled as Rafe explored her mouth. One large, warm hand moved to the back of her neck, holding her in place, while the other tightened low on her back, bringing her against the solid evidence of his need. His lips moved on hers, blocking her soft exclamation.

As she was drawn closer into the cradle of his thighs, Dani moaned, a soft sound of mingled astonishment and dismay. His hands kneaded in a gentle, deliberately sensuous action that kept her molded to the hard planes of his body.

Dani's sigh was a soft sound against his lips. Her hands loosened, sliding over his shoulders and meeting behind his neck. Her fingers touched his crisp, dark hair, luxuriating in the heavy pelt.

Rafe lifted his mouth and looked down into drowsy, green-gold eyes that were full of dazed contentment, then watched as the satisfaction mingled with uncertainty. The corners of his mouth quirked up in a half smile. His feisty love would hate it if she knew exactly how revealing her expression was.

Belatedly, Dani's eyes focused on the sheer male satisfaction gleaming in Rafe's eyes. Drawing in a shaky breath and mentally cursing the weakness that consumed her at this particular man's touch, she cleared her throat and said, "I don't think this is the smartest thing we've ever done."

His hands moved on her body, holding her still against him. "We've been heading for this since that night I found you in my office."

"*I* haven't," she denied. She was lying through her teeth, of course, but she was just beginning to realize the full danger of resting in his embrace. And the need to arm herself for the oncoming battle. "You have a very active imagination."

His hand tightened at the small of her back. "It's not my imagination that's bothering me," he stated evenly, his hard body expressing more than his words.

"Rafe," she protested, bracing her hands on his shoulders and beginning to press. "Let's not start something that's going to complicate our lives any more than they are already."

Touching her earlobe with his lips, he murmured, "Too late. We passed that stage a long time ago."

Shivering at the gentle caress, she shifted and muttered, her face pressed against his chest. Her words came out in a soft wail. "Rafe, I'm going back to Los Angeles and I'm not leaving part of me behind. I can't be more honest than that."

Rafe drew in a long breath. The movement of her soft, feminine curves against him was calling for more control than he had at the moment. He loosened his arms, aware of a startling sense of loss as soon as she

stepped away. "You're not going to make this easy, are
you?"

"What?"

"What we have between us."

She waved a hand nervously. "All we have here is a
little spontaneous combustion," she said. "If we leave
it alone, maybe it'll just go away."

"Not likely," he drawled. "But I'll tell you what
will happen."

"I don't think I want to hear this," she muttered.
Retreating until she backed into the counter, she
managed to move only a couple of inches. For all the
good it was doing, he was standing without touching
her. But she was ensnared in the warmth of his body,
in the clean, subtly spicy scent of his after-shave.

"You won't leave Carson City," he informed her.

Dani's gaze shot up from the button on his silk shirt
to the determined gleam in his eyes.

"You won't leave me."

Her eyes narrowed at his tone of absolute certainty.

"And you're going to be Mrs. Rafe Sutherland—"

"You're crazy!" she whispered, stunned at the
direction his words were taking.

"Before these two weeks are over."

"Is that all?" she asked politely, finally recovering
her voice.

He nodded. "For now. Except for this." He leaned
down and dropped a hard, swift kiss on her lips. Then
he turned and walked out of the kitchen, saying, "See
you later," over his shoulder.

Slowly she followed him through the house. The
front door closed quietly behind him while she was still
in the living room. Walking over to the window, she

edged back the lace curtain and watched his silver car shoot down the drive.

He was slipping, she decided, collapsing into a high-back chair. He hadn't ordered her to stay away from Munder's. He hadn't even tried to wring a promise out of her that she wouldn't join Nicholas. She was very carefully avoiding thoughts of what he *had* said, when Elise walked in with Nicholas.

"Do you know that your son is certifiable?" she asked the older woman pleasantly.

Elise stood in the doorway for a moment, enjoying the picture of Dani's bright yellow dress against the dark green velvet chair. Then she glanced at Nicholas, who promptly took the hint and excused himself. Entering the room, she dropped down on a nearby love seat, curling up in one corner. When it became apparent that Dani was not going to expand on that interesting statement, she smoothed the crease on her dark slacks and waited.

Trying to quell her amusement at Dani's expression of baffled irritation, she finally said, "Looks like you've just had your first encounter with the Sutherland syndrome."

Dani looked across at her suspiciously.

"Rafe's father was the same way."

"No one else could be that impossible," she stated flatly.

"Trust me," Elise said. "I wouldn't lie about it. I think it's something in the genes," she went on with a helpful look on her face.

"What is?"

"Rafe's attitude. His take-charge approach to life."

Dani's voice was dry. "Yes, he can be overwhelming, can't he?"

"A tad."

"That's an understatement if ever I heard one. Do you know what he had the gall to tell me?" she asked in complete exasperation.

"Having lived with his father for over thirty years, I can take a few guesses," Elise said, a wry expression on her face.

"That I'm going to stay here and marry him," Dani exploded wrathfully.

Elise's eyes were alight with humor. "Ah, that mad, impetuous youth!"

"Youth my...foot. He doesn't ask," Dani complained, "he *tells*."

"Yes, very much like his father," Elise said with a reminiscent smile. "And he has the same good taste."

"Elise! I don't think this is a joking matter."

"If it's any comfort, I doubt that he does, either."

Dani's eyes widened. "He can't be serious."

"Don't bet on it," Elise advised.

"I don't gamble."

"That's open to discussion," the older woman said dryly.

Hurriedly returning the discussion to its original point, Dani persisted, "Anyway, it's too soon. We only met a few days ago."

"According to family tradition, that doesn't have much bearing on the matter."

"What do you mean?" Dani asked with foreboding.

"I had known Daniel, Rafe's father, for four days when he made a similar pronouncement."

Dani winced. "What happened?"

"We were married ten days later."

There was a long, thoughtful pause before Dani asked, "Did you ever regret rushing into marriage?"

"With Daniel? Never." Her dark, steady eyes met Dani's. "Neither of us was a passive person and sometimes we fought like a couple of tigers. But life with him was exciting, tender, lusty, and far too short."

Dani looked away, allowing the other woman a few moments with her memories. Then, keeping her voice deliberately light, she said, "I thought you said 'family tradition.' That was a pretty short story."

"Ah. That's because I haven't told you about Grandfather Sutherland yet. He was even faster on the draw. He met and married within a week."

Dani studied the other woman morosely. This wasn't exactly what she wanted to hear. "Any more?" she reluctantly queried.

Elise nodded. "Great and great-great-grandfathers."

"How soon?" Dani asked in resignation.

"Nine and ten days, respectively."

"Anything else I should know?"

"One little detail," Elise said, amusement lurking in her dark eyes.

From the look on Elise's face, she knew she would regret asking. She asked, anyway. "What?"

"They were all one-woman men. They weren't easy men to live with, but they never strayed, and they kept their wives happy."

"What makes you so sure?"

A little smile curved Elise's lips. "Correspondence. Those were days when people kept journals and wrote voluminous letters. The Sutherland women all said the same thing—they had found men who protected, cherished and loved them.''

''And probably spent the biggest part of their time telling them what to do and how to do it,'' Dani grumbled, striking one feeble blow for the feminists. ''Didn't you mind being taken over body and soul?''

''By Daniel?''

Dani nodded. ''Didn't you resent having your wings clipped? Because, if he was anything like his son, you can't tell me he didn't try to take over the running of your life.''

''Oh, he tried, all right. And we fought. But I soon realized that the battles were about methods, not goals.''

''I beg your pardon?'' Dani's brows arched questioningly.

''Daniel didn't want me to change, or to give up any of my dreams,'' Elise said softly. ''He wanted to help me realize them.'' Grinning suddenly, she added, ''He just always thought his methods were the best. I disagreed, loudly and constantly. We had a marvelous time brawling.''

Temporarily giving up the battle, Dani said with a slow smile, ''He sounds like a wonderful man.''

Elise nodded and in a carefully casual voice said, ''His son is a carbon copy.''

Dani's mumbled reply was lost as she got up and restlessly paced around the room. Rafe was no blurred or smudged carbon copy. He exhibited all the earmarks of a well-defined original! Unaware of her deep sigh, she turned to the problem at hand.

''Did Rafe tell you what happened?''

''About Grady?'' Elise asked.

Dani nodded.

"Yes. This morning, before he came out here."

"What do you think he's going to do?"

Elise turned, watching Dani prowl around the room, straightening a curtain panel, rearranging fresh flowers in a large crystal vase. "Whatever he does, it will be effective," she said calmly.

"You sound awfully sure of that."

"I am. Another quality he inherited from his father is the ability to evaluate a problem. He's also willing to take whatever risk is involved in achieving the desired outcome."

Risk, again. There was always the aura of jeopardy around Rafe, she thought. "Good traits for a gambler, I suppose," she murmured, keeping her back turned to the other woman.

"Absolutely essential," Elise concurred briskly. "Those and the ability to count cards got him blackballed from the casinos in this state."

"What?" Dani turned, blank astonishment in her voice. Did that mean he *cheated*? She rejected the thought out of hand. Not Rafe.

"Blackballed," Elise repeated.

"I heard that part. What do you mean about the cards?"

"There are people who, either through training or sheer ability, can keep track of all the cards dealt in a game like blackjack. They're called 'card counters.' I think Rafe was born with the knack." With a shrug, she continued, "About five years ago, his reputation preceded him wherever he went. Soon he was barred from playing in the casinos."

"Is that legal?" Dani asked.

"It is in Nevada."

"I thought the whole structure of casinos was based on people gambling," Dani said with a frown of concentration. "Good heavens, they practically *give* hotel rooms away so people *will* gamble."

"Not to those who consistently beat the house odds," Elise said dryly.

"Oh. Obviously there's a lot more to this than meets the eye. Does anyone ever get away with cheating?"

"From which side?" Elise asked.

"Either."

"If a patron tries it, he's gently escorted from the premises."

"What about a dealer?"

"It's worth his job to try it," Elise said simply.

"Why?"

"A casino can't afford a dishonest employee," Elise explained carefully. "The Gaming Control Board polices casinos for infractions of gaming regulations. If it finds one, the casino can lose its license. For that reason alone, casino owners exhibit more concern about the protection of their customers than you'll find in other businesses. Their professional life is on the line."

"If everyone's reputation is so lily-white, how does Munder get away with the stuff he's doing?" Dani burst out. "It doesn't make sense."

"Why do you think Rafe is so determined to stop him? It could ruin the whole industry," Elise pointed out. "Rumors have been circulating for the past couple of months, confined mainly to the owners and key personnel. The control board has been sniffing around and hasn't found a thing."

"Suppose there isn't anything to find?" Dani asked slowly, a cold lump of doubt settling in her stomach as she wondered if Jim could have been mistaken.

"Possible. But not probable. It would be too coincidental to have that many disgruntled losers with the same story. The same one that your friend had. By the way, what do *you* think? He told you all about it."

"Jim's honest. I'd stake my life on that," Dani said, trying to be unbiased. "But he's green as grass where gambling is concerned. He *believes* he was cheated, but he hasn't got one shred of hard evidence."

"But you believe him?"

"Absolutely."

"There you are, then," Elise said with a shrug. "If you believe him, so would others. At least enough to raise doubts. Especially if more and more people produce the same story."

"So what are we going to do?" Dani asked, realizing that with that question she had—at least temporarily—just aligned herself with gamblers in general and one in particular.

"Well," Elise said with a supremely satisfied half smile, "I don't know about you, but I'm breaking into Munder's with Nicholas. And Rafe can take care of himself!"

Chapter Eight

Am I going to get another pop psychology lecture, or are we going to swim this time?"

Dani pinned a stern gaze on Rafe. Two dull, endless days had dragged by without a sign of him. Now he stood filling the doorway, patiently waiting for her to accept his invitation: a swim, lunch and, if they hadn't throttled each other by dinnertime, dinner. He was tempting and dangerous in faded denim cutoffs and a blue knit shirt stretched to the limit over his massive chest and shoulders, but Dani rationalized that since she had controlled herself this long, she could do it for another week or so.

"Swim," he promised, not looking at all like a man who had dropped a bombshell two days earlier before calmly walking out the door. "Yes or no?"

"Yes," she decided, swinging open the screen door. He stepped in and laced his fingers through hers, tugging her gently to his side.

"Zak hasn't tried to get rid of me lately," he commented as the door gave a pneumatic sigh and closed behind them. "Or steal my hat. I almost miss him."

"Tabitha's keeping him busy," Dani said, deliberately vague. At the sound of heavy footsteps on the porch stairs, they both swung around, Zak temporarily forgotten.

A young man, barely out of his teens, bounded up the steps. Catching sight of the couple inside the door, he skidded to a halt and shook his head, momentarily subduing a thatch of longish blond hair. "Is Art here?" he inquired.

Dani looked at him through the screening. "Art?" she asked blankly.

"Yeah. I'm sure this is the place. Wait a minute." He dug a hand in the front pocket of skintight jeans and pulled out a tattered piece of paper. "Here it is, Arthur Marlow."

Dani's gaze shifted down from the young man's creased cotton shirt to bare ankles showing above worn, grubby sneakers. Definitely not a courier from Arthur's brokerage firm. "Do you know him?" she asked.

The young man shook his head. "He's been leaving messages around for me. My friend took this one. Said he was a grumpy old geezer with a lot of white hair."

"Geezer," Dani repeated in a faint voice, visualizing the immaculately clad man upstairs who, although retired, never appeared in anything less formal than freshly pressed slacks and a dress shirt.

As if the thought had somehow nudged his subconscious, Arthur appeared at the top of the staircase. "Dani?" His testy voice was easily heard by the three at the door. "I'm expecting a young man with the peculiar name of Scanner to call. When he arrives, please let me know." His voice died away as he turned back to his room, but it was still sharp with disapproval as he added, "He's already late."

"Has to be him," Scanner said with a philosophical sigh. "Larry was right. He's a real grump."

"Scanner?" Rafe inquired with raised brows.

The young man nodded, a deprecating grin curving his lips. "Nickname," he said succinctly. "My name's Steve Connors." Observing Rafe's speculative glance, he explained. "Scanner, as in computers. Art's been putting out feelers for a hacker. I'm the best around."

Dani blinked at the casual statement. Scanner wasn't boasting, she saw, he was merely explaining things as he saw them. As they probably were.

"Arthur!" she called before the back of his white head disappeared. "Scanner's here. He just arrived."

He turned and looked down over the banister. "What are you doing down there?" he demanded, squinting to see through the screen. "We've got work to do."

"I'm not working for you yet," Scanner called up, nodding as Rafe opened the door.

"I can't very well employ someone who can't be found," Arthur grumbled. "You *are* for hire, aren't you?" His tone implied that anyone who didn't wear socks should not look gift horses in the mouth.

"That all depends," Scanner said, taking the stairs two at a time, eyeing the redoubtable old man steadily, "on how interesting the project is."

Arthur's expression changed to one of avid anticipation. His sudden sharklike smile startled the younger man. "I don't think you'll have any problems with that part of it," he promised. "Come into my office." A closing door shut off the sounds of any further communication between the two men.

Dani looked up at Rafe and shrugged. Both knew enough about the growing breed of computer whizzes to venture a guess as to what was being discussed in the room upstairs. "I'll get my suit," she said.

This time when they passed the discreet sign that announced the beginning of Rafe's property Dani paid more attention. The road was private, tree-lined and curving. She had already fallen in love with the rambling white house. Gambling obviously paid well, she thought, trying to control her expressive face.

"Judging from those sidelong glances, you're dying to say something," Rafe said, pulling to the side of the house and parking the car. "Why don't you just do it and get it over with?"

"I heard you've been blackballed by the casinos," she said bluntly.

"You heard right," he agreed easily, opening her door and taking her hand. "But, believe it or not, it's not a stigma. It's not like being cited for indecent exposure, you know."

She slid out of the car and walked beside him toward the house. "What *is* it like?"

He shrugged, as if trying to displace an annoying insect. "Inconvenient, more than anything. I have a hell of a time getting together a friendly game of poker," he said whimsically.

"But why did they do it?"

"Because I was beating the odds. Consistently."

"But that's not fair!"

He shrugged again. "Maybe not, but they did it. It would be the same thing if you were taking part in some academic competition and were disqualified for having a photographic memory. No difference at all." Opening the front door, he said, "I want you to see the house first, this time."

"In case I pack my bag and leave early again?"

"Something like that," he said with an easy grin. "Welcome to Sutherlands."

She caught her breath as she preceded him through the door. His words brought back the scene at the pool, exactly as he'd intended them to.

Fortunately the house itself was a perfect distraction. "Rafe, it's lovely!" she exclaimed. And it was. It was warm and masculine without being overpowering. Large windows, covered with sheer curtains, took advantage of the early afternoon light. Wide-planked floors gleamed where jewel-toned throw rugs didn't cover them. The furniture was solid oak, in warm, complimentary colors, made to suit a large man. All it needed, she decided, was a touch of flowers here and there and a few magazines lying around.

His large hand, lightly resting at the small of her back, guided her into the next room. "My office."

"Oh, Rafe," she breathed. It was another spacious room, but in this one, the back wall was one large window. She walked around a massive desk to take in the panoramic scene outside. "It's the valley with all the cows," she said in pleased surprise.

Rafe followed her. "I thought I should take advantage of the view," he drawled, satisfied with her reaction.

She turned, gazing around the comfortable, book-lined room. "It looks like you spend a lot of time in here."

"Um-hmm." He glanced down at her, then over to the deep turquoise sofa in front of the fireplace. In the past few days, he had pictured her lying there, her hair spread like warm honey over the cushion, wearing only the soft warm glow of the fire. For a man who considered himself pragmatic and rather unimaginative, he had produced a particularly lifelike image. And her presence in the room wasn't helping. Moving away, he prowled restlessly to the other side of the room, absently running his fingers over a row of books.

Pulled by some inner tension emanating from Rafe, Dani's alert gaze followed him. After a few taut moments she asked, "Are you going to show me the rest of the house?"

"I think that's a good idea," he muttered. Leading the way, he took her on a whirlwind tour. When they reached his bedroom, her eyes widened briefly at the size of his bed—it seemed enormous. But, then, so were his room and all the rest of the furniture. When they finally came to a halt in the kitchen, her overwhelming impressions were of space and light, beautifully grained wood demanding to be touched and deep, vibrant colors.

"That's the end of the ten-cent tour," he announced, opening the refrigerator and pulling out two cold beers and holding them up with a questioning look.

She shook her head and, peering over his shoulder, pointed to a chilled bottle of sauvignon blanc. "I would have paid the extra fifteen cents if the quarter tour had been slower."

"Too fast?" he asked, carefully pouring wine into a stemmed glass.

"A little."

He turned and handed her the glass, his eyes steady on hers. "Sorry," he said. "I'm usually more... patient."

Dani blinked over the edge of the glass. The infinitesimal pause before his last word was deliberate. It was also provocative, baiting and extremely annoying. And she wouldn't touch any part of it with asbestos gloves.

Rafe waited, watching the varied expressions chase across her face, then read her final decision. Too bad. She wasn't going to bite. Ah, well. He had all day. There was no rush. Raising the perspiring bottle to his lips, he swallowed. "Ready for a swim?"

His sudden slashing grin startled her. "That's what I came for," she said, her eyes gleaming with sudden challenge. She was tired of feeling off-balance around him. She was also exasperated by the sensation of being in over her head when she wasn't even in the pool!

This time Rafe didn't allow her the luxury of lazing in the water. As soon as she slid in, he commandeered her into swimming laps.

"Wait a minute," she panted, stopping in the deep end, clinging to the side after losing count of the number of lengths they had gone. Rafe had adapted himself to her pace instead of swimming at his usual breakneck speed, so he was right beside her. "I can't keep this up forever."

"We've got time," he said, treading water beside her. "I'm in no hurry."

Dani tilted her head, looking up at him thoughtfully, her hazel eyes narrowing. That was the second time. This seemed to be his day for uttering cryptic statements. And his bland expression wasn't a bit convincing. He knew exactly what he was doing!

Rafe turned, reaching up and planting his hands on the edge of the pool, one on either side of her head, his arms forming a loose cage around her. Dani looked up into dark, steady eyes. The waiting, expectant look in them set her blood roaring like a freight train and made the water feel startlingly chilly next to her suddenly overheated skin. Without even touching her, he could cause her body to tighten into one aching mass.

The man was a mystery to her, she reflected, backing up cautiously against the side of the pool. Although he hadn't tried to hustle her into bed, he had left her with no doubts that when it happened—and his nonverbal messages assured her that it surely would—it would be an occasion to remember. His unreadable gaze alternately promised and threatened, leaving her in a palpitating state reminiscent of old-time movie heroines.

Just his unblinking gaze was enough to set off the incipient panic that never seemed far beneath the surface when he was around, and to paralyze her tongue when it would be most useful. She could never think of a thing to say when he closed in on her like this. Somehow words seemed such an ineffectual weapon against his potential arsenal.

"Rafe," she began, making an effort, anyway. His legs drifted against her, thwarting her poor attempt before it even got off the ground. She sucked in a deep breath and felt his dark gaze settle on her breasts with the impact of a physical touch. Briefly she closed her eyes. I'm an independent, mature woman, she reminded herself. I run a business of my own and I don't fall apart at a man's touch. Peering up through her lashes at the tan planes of his face, she added, and I also lie a lot!

Rafe lowered his head, brushing his lips against the corner of her mouth, absorbing a drop of water that had settled there. Before he even touched her, he was aware of the tension in her slender body. His mouth drifted along her shoulder and pure male satisfaction surged through him when she shivered. She could talk until she was blue in the face, but she'd never convince him that she was indifferent.

"We have time, Dani" he muttered darkly against her satiny skin, "but why waste it? You want me as much as I want you, don't you?"

"There's more to life than wanting," she gasped, twitching her shoulder as his mustache brushed toward her collarbone.

"Don't you?"

"Things like responsibilities and—"

He went to work on her other shoulder. "Don't you?"

"Duty and—"

Touching her earlobe with his mouth, he persisted, *"Don't* you?"

"And promises, and..." She forgot whatever other virtuous traits she had meant to mention. He was, purely and simply, driving her crazy. How could a woman think while undergoing this particular version of water torture? "Damn you, Rafe Sutherland," she said with a sigh, slipping her arms around his neck.

He tightened his grip on the decking, gently pinning her between his hard body and the glassy tiles of the pool.

Dani looked up, startled, as he settled against her. His gambler's face, trained to remain expressionless, was one thing. The instinctive movement of his body was entirely another. He did indeed want her! That disarmed her as nothing else could have. Her defenses, drawn to fortify her against the advances of a man accustomed to playing in the big league, dissolved at the naked sign of vulnerability.

His lips hovered over hers. "I need you, Dani."

Then take me! she wanted to say. One last remnant of sanity held back the words. Instead she tangled her hands in his hair and tugged until his mouth met and covered her parted lips. That first bit of initiative was her last.

The kiss was a leisurely, hungry caress that she felt down to the tips of her toes. The damp heat of their mouths dazed her, radiated outward, sending a satiny weakness through her limbs. When his legs snared her, drawing her into the cradle of his thighs, she sighed against his lips. Later, she would face the complications of this moment. Right now, there was only Rafe's mouth and strong, heated body.

Taking a deep breath, he tucked Dani's head under his chin. His voice was a husky bit of enchantment as he murmured, "Dani."

She smiled against his throat. "What?"

"Just . . . Dani."

"Oh," she whispered in contentment, neither knowing nor caring what they were talking about.

He looked down at her dreamy face and cursed his sudden attack of scruples. He could make her his, right here and now. She knew it and wasn't doing a thing to stop him. Damning his early civilized upbringing and the unsettled problems between them, he gently unwound her arms from around his neck.

"Hold on a minute," he said, framing one of her hands to the rounded edge of the pool and pressing it with his own to ensure her grip. "I'll be right back." He pushed off from the side and surged through the water.

"Rafe?" she said huskily, watching him swim away. She had the feeling that the act was symbolic, an augury, but he was back before she could examine her thoughts.

He hauled himself out of the water with an easy, masculine grace, then leaned and pulled Dani up beside him. "Sun or shade?" he inquired.

"Sun," she said vaguely. "For a while."

He draped his arm around her shoulders and led her to a large, striped, inflated mattress the size of a blanket. Then he released her and watched as, with all the graceful meticulousness of a cat, she settled on one side. Still wrapped in thought, she sat with knees bent, one arm braced behind her, the other resting on her knees.

She glanced down as Rafe dropped on his back in a magnificent sprawl beside her, his shoulder touching her hip, his legs stretched out behind her. The bright sun highlighted his springy mat of chest hair, turning it several shades lighter.

"Comfortable?" he asked, assessing her remote expression.

"Just fine," she lied, trying to ignore her body's various bereft complaints.

"When are you going to marry me?"

The lazily put, outrageous question had her glaring down at him. "Are you crazy?"

At least, he thought, his eyes gleaming darkly behind black lashes, he had caught her attention.

"You're going to end up in my bed," he stated calmly, closing his eyes and shifting fractionally closer to her. "I just thought you might want to legitimize it."

"Crazy," she repeated, her heart jumping at the thought. "As a bedbug."

"Just thought I'd mention it."

"It'd never work," she assured him, perversely annoyed that he wasn't pursuing the subject with more energy. Even though marriage between them wasn't on the books, it was rather deflating when a man couldn't work up a bit more zeal.

"Sure it would." His hand cupped her shoulder for a moment, then his fingers lightly traced a pattern across her back between the straps of her suit. "You'd find a way to make it work."

"*I* would?" she said in disbelief, sitting up straight to escape his questioning fingers. "It's your idea. Why should I put any effort into the whole thing?"

"Well, if you want our children to be born on the wrong side of the blanket, I guess it's okay with me," he said doubtfully.

Dani's lashes dropped, concealing the quick shaft of pain that darkened her hazel eyes. She knew with heartbreaking certainty that she would never carry Rafe Sutherland's child in her body. Before she could do more than clear her throat, Elise's voice called out.

"Rafe? Are you decent?" After a pause, she said in a lower voice, obviously to someone beside her, "I've yelled like this for the past couple of years, ever since I barged in while he was skinny-dipping. *Rafe*. Are you there?"

"Skinny-dipping?" Dani asked, relieved that she could still curve her lips in some semblance of a smile.

Muffling a groan, Rafe rolled to his feet and pulled Dani up next to him. "Mothers," he said in disgust. "This—" he pointed to his brief, dark suit "—is for your benefit. When I'm alone, I swim in the nude."

"Thanks for the concession," she said dryly.

"Rafe!"

"There are times when I think she could win a hog-calling contest," he muttered, wincing. "It's safe," he called, looking toward the gate. "You can come in."

"Hi, darling," Elise said breezily, coming over and standing on tiptoe to kiss him on the cheek. Nicholas stood at her side, his dark eyes taking in Dani's high color and Rafe's impatient expression.

The two men nodded politely while Elise explained that she and Nicholas had been out for a drive. "I told Nicholas that if you were home, you'd give us something to drink."

Rafe herded them into the shaded area and seated Dani at a glass-topped table. Nicholas did the same for Elise before Rafe could move around to her.

"Do you want another glass of wine?" he asked Dani.

She nodded and Elise opted for the same.

"I'll help you," Nicholas said quietly to Rafe.

Two pairs of feminine eyes watched the two men walk into the house. Although Rafe towered over the older man, both moved with catlike grace: Rafe with the tight-knit coordination and strength of a natural athlete, Nicholas with the smooth effortlessness of a dancer.

The women sighed and looked ruefully at each other.

"Well," Elise demanded after a moment, smoothing her khaki skirt over her knees, "did I arrive in the

nick of time, or will you never forgive me for inter-
rupting?''

"I think it was time for the cavalry to come charging over the hill," Dani said slowly.

"Good."

Dani smiled with genuine amusement. "You know,
I *could* be forgiven for thinking that you're hell-bent
on rescuing your son."

"God forbid," Elise said piously. "You think I'd
mess up the first serious opportunity I've had of getting a grandchild? I'll be happy to welcome you into
the family. Delighted, as a matter of fact. I just think
you deserve a fighting chance to escape, if you really
want to."

"Serious discussions are prohibited at poolside
parties," Rafe said, reaching over Dani's shoulder and
setting her drink on the table. His brows drew together as he aimed a speculative glance at the two
women.

"Exactly what I was telling Dani," Elise lied without a blink, smiling at Nicholas as he handed her a
glass.

After the two men sat down, Nicholas lifted his can
of beer in a toast. "To success."

"To knowing what it is," Rafe added, touching his
can to Dani's glass.

"To enjoying it when it comes along," Elise said
blithely.

"To making sure it's what you really want," Dani
said, looking at her glass, aware of Rafe stiffening
beside her.

"You're missing the excitement at the house,"
Nicholas quietly said to Dani, breaking the small, taut
silence.

Smothering a sigh of relief, she darted a quick smile at him and asked, "What's happening?"

"For one thing," Elise broke in, "there's a strange young man without socks holed up with Arthur. They were eating lunch while we were there and they might as well have been speaking a foreign language. Couldn't understand a word they were saying. Isn't that right?" she demanded of Nicholas.

Nicholas smiled, both at the memory and Elise's bright face. He nodded.

"What else?" Dani asked.

"The telephone is ringing off the hook."

"Who for?"

"It's a toss-up between Billy Bob and Emily," Elise said. "They're elbowing each other out of the way trying to get to it first."

"Who's calling them?" Dani wanted to know, uncomfortably aware of Rafe's silence.

"High rollers and Save the Whalers," said the irrepressible Elise. "They're all coming to visit and seem to be confirming times and dates."

"And Tabitha?" Dani asked cautiously, not sure she wanted to hear.

"I can't quite figure out *what* she's doing. Can you?" Elise asked Nicholas. He smiled and shook his head, perfectly content to sit and watch her.

"What does it look like?" Dani asked reasonably.

"She's teaching Zak something. He keeps falling down dead and making terrible faces." The other three smiled at the beatific expression on her face. "I tell you, Dani, I've never had so much fun in my entire life."

Elise looked like a little girl who had just been given the key to a candy store, Dani thought. The silver halo of curls looked absurdly out of place atop the youthful, vivid face. Nicholas, she decided after a quick glance, thought so, too.

"And what are you doing to add to the excitement?" Rafe asked the older man.

Nicholas shrugged. "I'm the dull one," he said with a small smile.

He thinks that's really true, Dani realized with a start.

"Don't you believe it," Elise told her son emphatically. "He's collected some absolutely fascinating information about the Golden Boar. And he's been teaching me to read blueprints."

Rafe nodded impassively, thinking of the roll of drawings in the casino office. Once, when he had shown them to her, she had looked for all of thirty seconds, brushed imaginary dust from her hands and informed him that they were boring.

"And what are you learning from them?"

"Everything!" she said with enthusiasm. "Secret doors and concealed windows, all sorts of things. You know," she said thoughtfully to Rafe, "I'm afraid we've gotten very dull over the years."

Rafe looked from his mother to Nicholas, wondering just how much the older man had to do with her revitalization. Nicholas met his unblinking gaze, not backing down an inch.

Dani noted the exchange of glances with interest. Nicholas, she could have told Rafe, might be quiet, but he was absolutely relentless. Once he decided that he wanted something, he never gave up until he got it.

His mother, Rafe decided abruptly, could take care of herself. He had his own problems. He leaned back in his chair, his arm brushing lightly against Dani's.

Casually he laced his fingers with hers, forcing her to reach for her glass with her left hand. She flushed, aware of Elise's interested gaze, as she did so. Making an effort to remain cool, she tugged in what she hoped was an unobtrusive manner. Rafe's grasp tightened, not enough to hurt, but enough to ensure that she wouldn't escape.

Nicholas, observing the byplay, tilted his beer can again. A tug of wry humor warmed his dry voice. "Success," he murmured.

Rafe's voice sounded surprisingly like the older man's. "Success."

"Success," Elise bubbled, upending her glass with a flourish.

Dani glared at the glass near her unencumbered left hand and remained silent.

Chapter Nine

Dani's first impression of Jed Munder was that he was not the sort of man a girl took home to dinner in hopes of receiving unqualified parental approval. Her feelings didn't change in the short time she was with him. His hands were clammy, he called her "little lady," and his smile never once reached his eyes.

She almost pitied him. If it weren't for Jim and all his other victims, she would have. He would never fit in Rafe's milieu. He would never wear his clothes with the same casual elegance. He would never belong. His clothes were expensive, she noted, but already wilting on his stocky frame. He would always be the man who fought his way out of one environment only to find that he had no better place to go.

She stood aside, looking owlish in her outsize reading glasses, listening while Emily uncharacteristically dithered. Emily had decreed that she wear the glasses. "It's part of the overall impression," she'd said, adding bluntly, "when you wear them, you don't look clever enough to outsmart anyone." Considering that they were the glasses she wore in her office, Dani resolved that the first thing she was going to do when she returned to Los Angeles was make an appointment with her optometrist.

Emily's dithering was also part of the master plan. "I want to present the image of a brainless do-gooder," she'd informed Dani, practically quivering with excitement. In the years since Emily had seen and delighted in the intricacies of *The Sting*, she had known in her heart of hearts that her talents would one day be called upon for such an operation. "No one would ever suspect such a person of being involved in a scam," she had added. Well, in Dani's opinion, she was doing an unparalleled job.

"Mr. Munder," she trilled, fluttering her eyelashes up at the perspiring man and smoothing her wild, brown hair. "You don't know how honored we are to launch your new community service program. Especially since whales aren't exactly a first consideration here in Carson City." Dani, who had once been privileged to watch Emily trumpet orders into a bullhorn, chain herself to the fence of a prospective nuclear site and be hauled away feet-first by the police, watched the performance with a great deal of pleasure.

"Happy to be of help," he assured her, running his hands through his thinning, reddish hair with a harassed gesture.

"Tabitha will be bringing her friends here for publicity pictures later. It is this afternoon, isn't it?" she asked Dani, waving a lace hankie with a helpless air. Without waiting for a reply, she turned back to Munder. "My granddaughter," she confided in a portentous voice, blinking rapidly. "She keeps my life uncluttered so I may attend to the larger concerns."

Dani concentrated on looking efficient and colorless. Apparently she succeeded.

"Yes, yes," Munder agreed, casting a hasty glance at her.

"Dani, dear," Emily said, "come meet this wonderful man."

The two reluctantly shook hands.

The wonderful man was apparently not comfortable around women, Dani decided. He muttered, "Er, yes, yes," and quickly withdrew his hand. As soon as he turned away, she wiped hers on the back of her skirt.

Twenty minutes later, Emily was confirming the entire set of plans for the third time. "Now, let me see if I have everything straight," she said, beginning to count on her fingers. "The banquet is—" she looked helplessly at Dani.

"Friday."

"At—"

"Eight."

"And we're serving—"

"One hundred."

Moving on to her last finger, she said, "And the awards are being presented at—"

"Ten o'clock."

"Wonderful!" She beamed at the man beside her. "Isn't she wonderful?"

"Wonderful," he agreed hastily, looking at his watch. "Well, ladies, if there's nothing else I can do for you," he began, "I'll—"

"Oh, Mr. Munder," Emily gasped. "There is one small favor I'd like to ask."

He exhaled sharply and forced his lips upward in a smile. "Anything at all," he said, his gaze shifting restlessly around the room.

"My little Dani has arranged so many of these events for me that the novelty has quite worn off."

He waited, swallowing a yawn, his eyes bugging and watering.

"And I wanted to plan a little treat for her. With your permission, of course. And your help."

"I have an, uh, appointment Friday evening," he said. "But if one of my staff could be of..."

"Just the thing!" Emily said, beaming. "And, of course, I didn't mean to suggest that *you* would do it personally. I would never dream of imposing on such a busy—"

"What do you want?" The words came slowly and, Dani swore, between clenched teeth.

"A tour!"

"Tour?" He cocked his head as if there were something wrong with his hearing. "Of the casino?"

"Yes!" Emily held her hands in a prayerful pose. "Would you mind?"

He looked out past the uniform rows of slot machines with their blinking lights and clattering coins. "This is open to anyone," he said, as if explaining the facts of life to a dimwit. "She doesn't need permission." Once again he glanced at his watch.

"But that's the trouble," Emily said, clamping her hand on his arm and holding him in place. "Dani likes to see *background*. She likes kitchens and offices and stockrooms and—"

"Fine," Munder interrupted ruthlessly. He reached in his breast pocket and pulled out a business card. He scribbled on it and thrust it into Emily's hand. "Give

this to the banquet hostess and she'll take care of it.
Your granddaughter can go anywhere she likes!" Before she could think of anything else, he turned on his
heel and strode away.

"That was like taking candy from a baby," Emily
murmured, watching his receding back. "No challenge at all." She stuffed the lace hankie in her purse
with an absent gesture. "Here." She handed Dani the
card. "It's your passport to the place."

On Wednesday morning Billy Bob, Tabitha, Arthur,
Emily, Nicholas and Dani sat around the kitchen table with copies of the early edition of the newspaper.
There was an appreciative silence as they took in the
spread on the front page. Jed Munder was in every
picture, surrounded by luminaries of the entertainment world. His smile was almost as wide as Zak's.

"How on earth did you get all these people together?" Dani asked.

"They owed me," Tabitha said succinctly. "This is
how I collected."

"Owed you for what?" Billy Bob asked, blue eyes
bright with curiosity.

She waved a hand. "This and that." When she saw
that he wasn't going to give up, she said, "I've done
benefits with all of them at one time or another.
Where animals are concerned, they don't have the
sense God gave a goat. At various times and places,
I've kept them all from having chunks taken out of
their hides."

Dani dropped the paper on the table. "But where
did you find them?"

Tabitha grinned. "Look in the entertainment section. They're all appearing in Vegas, Reno or Tahoe.

It was just a matter of collecting them and getting them back in time for the evening shows. And Billy Bob took care of that. He sent out planes and limos," she said, answering Dani's mute inquiry.

"Billy!" Dani turned to him, concern drawing her brows together. "That must have cost a fortune."

"Not nearly as much as the jet he's chartering to bring in my Whalers," Emily said dryly.

"*Billy.*" Dani strung the word out to three syllables.

"And he's picking up their hotel tabs."

Dani held up her hand for silence. "Wait just a minute, folks. I think this thing is getting entirely out of hand. What do you *mean*, a jet from California?"

"How did you think they were getting here for the banquet?" Emily asked reasonably.

"I didn't. Think, I mean. I guess I just thought they were coming on their own, straggling in one by one. It just never occurred to me that anyone was going to have to finance this thing."

"Dani—" Emily looked at her pityingly, as if she had escaped adolescence without learning one of the basic fundamentals of life. "You don't ignore what the gods drop in your lap. Jed Munder wants to be a philanthropist. I'm giving him the opportunity. He's supplying the room *and* the banquet. He's even invited a few people with money to burn who are looking for a cause to support. Tax deductible, of course. I'm supplying the people and picking up some cash for the Whalers. What could be better? All Billy has to do is convince his tax man that *his* expenses are deductible." She stopped, pleased that she had tied up the loose ends so neatly.

"But Billy shouldn't be paying for all this," Dani protested. "It's probably already cost more than Jim's debt! And what if it *isn't* deductible?"

"Well, honey, that don't matter." Billy patted her arm with a work-roughened hand. "I ain't had so much fun since I was a Texas Ranger."

"You were born and bred in Oklahoma," she reminded him.

"That's right," he said, a teasing glint in his faded blue eyes. "Must have been the vigilantes."

She was opening her mouth to voice another protest, when Arthur impatiently interrupted. "The money isn't important, Dani. What we're doing *is*."

Closing her mouth with a snap, she leaned back and looked at her adopted family. Billy Bob, wiry and whipcord thin, was explaining complacently that his high-rolling friends would be in that evening. Emily, obviously in her glory, gave her progress report. Arthur, white brows beetling with enthusiasm, was involving himself in one of the family escapades for the first time. Tabitha impatiently waited to jump in, and Nicholas sat quietly, waiting for the din to die down before he took charge.

Arthur was right. The money wasn't important, for the simple reason that every one of them had plenty of it. Arthur had seen to that. Years before, he had set up a portfolio for each of them. True to form, they had each entrusted him with the care and feeding of their investments. As a result, they were all quite comfortably situated. Billy, of course, had a head start with his oil money, Nicholas from his life before retirement. The others had begun with modest sums, but with one of the country's most perspicacious stockbrokers in their corner, their accounts had blossomed quite nicely. No, money wasn't important. And yes, she agreed again, looking at their anticipation, their vitality, what they were doing, *was*.

"So me and Bobby Joe and Red and Earl Dean are going to meander down to the Golden Boar tonight and tomorrow night," Billy explained. "By Friday, when we bring in the big money, they'll be used to us."

"I made hotel reservations for the Whalers, picked up the plaques to be presented and had press packets printed," Emily reported.

Arthur looked up from some scribbled notes. "Scanner said—"

"Can't you make that boy wear socks?" Emily asked, concern momentarily distracting her. "He's going to get a roaring case of athlete's foot. Or is it feet?" she asked, turning to Tabitha.

"Who cares?" she asked in turn. "I don't care if he's covered in fungus if he can help us. Can he?" she queried, turning to Arthur.

"Scanner *says*," he repeated with enough emphasis to quiet them all, "that by Friday, he should be able to get into their files." He turned to Dani. "Is Jim's record the only one you want deleted?"

Squinting her eyes in thought, she said slowly, "That might be a little obvious. If they ever figure out what we did, that is. How about seeing if there's a number or code by his name. If there is, erase everyone with the same code. And while Nicholas gets Jim's IOU, if they are all filed together, he can grab the rest of them."

Arthur's smile was little more than a preoccupied twitch of his lips. He jotted something quickly on his growing stack of notes. "Anything else?" he muttered.

"You're the financial whiz around here," Dani reminded him. "As long as you're tiptoeing through his accounts, see if you can find anything incriminating and get some hard copy of it. Who knows, if this doesn't work, we may have to resort to blackmail."

"O ye of little faith," Nicholas murmured.

"Sorry, darling." She flashed him a smile. "I've never taken part in a strategy session before, and it's making me nervous."

"The first time's always the worst," he assured her.

"Ummm," she mumbled. If she survived this experience, she wasn't sure she'd be back for a repeat performance.

"Rafe was right about one thing," Nicholas admitted, ignoring her chickenhearted reply. "Munder's security is good."

Coming from Nicholas, that was almost the equivalent of Houdini admitting defeat, packing up his chains and trunks and heading for home. Five faces swiveled toward him in concern.

"But there's always room for improvement," he said, his quick, confident, slashing grin reassuring them. "There are a couple of spots—"

With a suddenness that caught them all by surprise, the kitchen door was flung open and banged against the wall. Dani noted with disgust that she was the only one who gave a guilty start.

"I escaped!" Elise announced dramatically. She looked elegant in her jade silk blouse and gray slacks.

Nicholas rose, his face softening as he looked at her flushed face and deliciously tousled hair. "From whom?" he asked with a small smile.

"My son, the jailer. I swear to God," she said, collapsing in a chair and looking thoroughly pleased with herself, "he's going to drive me mad. If he isn't camping on my front porch, he's calling me every ten minutes."

Right on cue, the telephone rang.

"It's him," Elise groaned. Her eyes laughed at the others. "I haven't been gone thirty minutes and he's tracked me down. You get it, Dani," she ordered, nodding at the insistent phone. "Talk to him. Keep him occupied." Just as Dani reached for it, she said frantically, "Saturday. I told him we were going to Munder's on Saturday."

Dani looked at the telephone as if it were a hissing snake. It might be the IRS telling her she was going to be audited, she thought hopefully. It wasn't.

"Dani?"

"Hi, Rafe." *Saturday?* What on earth was Elise up to? "Now that you've called, your family's accounted for," she said, taking the battle to his camp. "Your mom just dropped in for a cup of coffee and to admire Munder's pictures on the front page of the paper."

"She's there?" he asked, sounding oddly disconcerted.

"Um-hmm. As a matter of fact, she just walked in. Want to talk to her?"

"No, that's okay. Actually—" he paused as if the conversation were not going as he had planned "—I wanted to know if you're free for dinner. Saturday."

"Saturday," she repeated, and was distracted by Elise frantically waving her hands and mouthing, "Busy! Busy!"

"Sorry, but I'm busy," she said obediently. Wincing at the bald statement, she added quickly, "I mean, I promised Nicholas that I'd do something for him."

Elise beamed in approval; Nicholas just shook his head. "What I mean," she amended her statement carefully, "is—"

"I know just what you mean," Rafe said grimly. "You're going to Munder's on Saturday."

"That's about the size of it," she admitted with a shrug. "What about Friday?" she asked out of sheer perversity, not knowing what she'd do if he agreed.

Instead there was an interesting silence on his end of the line. "I've got an appointment on Friday," he said finally.

"Oh. Then maybe Sunday."

"Yeah. Dani?" he said after a long pause.

"Yes?"

"You know I don't want you to get involved at Munder's, don't you?"

"I know," she agreed, nodding. "But my mind's made up. It has been for some time." Tensing at the continued silence, she waited for his explosion. It didn't come.

"I'll call you before Sunday," he said abruptly, and hung up.

She replaced the receiver, puzzled by the intriguing silences and his lack of response. "He's up to something," she said to Elise.

"I'm sure of it, but he plays his cards pretty close to his chest. We won't find out until he's ready to tell us."

"Why Saturday?" Dani asked, hoping to solve at least one riddle.

"Because I *know* he isn't going to sit and meekly watch us—" she pointed to herself and Dani "—get involved with Jed Munder. I figured that if he was driven to kidnapping, he'd wait until Saturday morning. And by that time, it would be all over but the shouting.''

"But surely he's seen this," Tabitha said, holding up the paper. "It says everything's happening on Friday."

"It says the Save the Whale banquet is on Friday, and that you're bringing Zak in for a performance," Elise calmly pointed out. "That would be the logical time for us to create some diversion for Nicholas—and Rafe is nothing if not logical. But—" she raised limpid eyes "—would his own mother lie to him?"

"Positively Machiavellian," Arthur said, surprised respect warming his voice.

Nicholas's dark eyes gleamed with tender amusement. Then he removed the newspapers and dropped a large, detailed drawing in the center of the table. "Gather around. We've got a lot of work to do," he said briskly.

"Synchronize your watches."

"Even Paul Newman couldn't have planned this better."

"Imagine, if I had listened to Rafe, I would have missed this!"

"Zak and I are as ready as we'll ever be."

"This is *better* than the vigilantes."

"Scanner says we might even play around with their security system."

"I'm going back to L.A. and pretend this was all a bad dream," Dani announced, wondering what other surprises Arthur and his protégé had up their sleeves.

"Miss Clayton?"

Dani turned away from her position at the door of the noisy banquet room and automatically restored her sliding glasses to the bridge of her nose. "Yes."

The man was wearing formal evening wear, but something about him reminded her of a friend who worked as a bouncer in a very tough neighborhood. He held up the card with Munder's scribbled signature. "I'm Sam Farley. Connie—" he gestured to where the hostess was standing "—said I should show you around the place."

"Wonderful, Mr. Farley. Just let me say a word to my grandmother, and I'll be right with you."

His massive shrug was not ungracious, just unconcerned. That was all to her advantage, she decided. The more thoroughly bored he was, the less attention he would pay to anything she chose to do.

"I'll be here," he promised, leaning against the wall. "And it's not 'mister' anything. Just call me 'Sam.'"

She nodded and made her way over to where Emily was seated. "I'm going now," she said in a low voice. They both looked at their watches. One minute until ten.

"I wish I were," Emily said, openly envious. "But I've still got to give a long, boring speech, present an award to practically everyone here and generally drag this thing out. You have an hour to get into position. And Dani..."

"Yes?" Dani looked up from her nervous scrutiny of her watch.

"Have fun, honey!"

She meant it, Dani reflected, turning back toward her indifferent escort. She really meant it! The whole thing was giving her an ulcer, and this fire-eating old woman was telling her to enjoy herself. She hated to admit it, even to herself, but knowing all of the risks involved had definitely dulled her appetite for adventure. Especially since she'd had a good look at Jed Munder's security force. Some of them were just one step removed from the missing link. Of course, all Rafe's warnings and comments about shallow graves under cactus plants hadn't helped. It gave her an entirely new—and unwelcome—insight into her personality to realize that her six senior citizens were having the time of their lives while she walked around with a frozen ball of apprehension in her stomach.

"Where first?" Sam asked, straightening as she approached.

"How about the kitchens?"

Forty minutes later, Dani has seen enough kitchen appliances and linen closets to last her a lifetime. The same could be said for back stairways. She had edged nearer her goal when she asked to see the empty business offices, specifically accounting. Jed Munder's office had been a revelation. It was done in knotty pine with animal heads adorning the walls. Animals with large horns.

Now, after taking a quick peek at her watch, she said, "I saw a movie once about a casino."

"Was it any good?" Sam asked with patent disinterest.

"No. As a matter of fact, it was lousy. But one thing in it caught my eye. They showed a room with a lot of TV monitors. It looked like the people in there could keep an eye on the whole operation."

"Oh, yeah. Security. I worked up there for a while. Couldn't stand it."

"Too much excitement?" she hazarded.

He shook his head. "Not enough. You stand around and watch TV screens until you're cross-eyed. I had to get out where I could move around."

"That's what I want to see next," Dani told him.

Sam stopped and looked down at her. "You sure?" he asked. "Wouldn't you rather go down to one of the lounges and see a show?"

Dani shook her head, aiming a wide smile at him. "I'm sorry, Sam. I'm really interested in this. I won't bother anyone, and it's the last thing I'll ask to see. So if you'll just take me there and tell me how it works, you'll be off the hook."

Sighing, he said, "Okay, lady. Mr. Munder said to take you wherever you wanted to go. So we go to security." He punched an elevator button and waved her in as the doors opened.

The ride—all two floors of it—seemed endless to Dani. Her idea, the master plan, which had seemed so brilliant at the time, now had as much vigor as a popped balloon. The fact that she was about to become the hub of the whole scheme was not the adrenaline-pumping event she had thought it would be. On the contrary. She would give a year of her portfolio profits to have just a smidgen of Elise's exuberance. Or Emily's confidence. Or even Arthur's preoccupation. Anything but the overwhelming sense of responsibility and fear of failure that now consumed her. At this point, she decided, she didn't care if feminism was set back a decade, she'd give her *entire* portfolio to see Rafe bearing down on her, intent on hustling her out of the place.

"Here we are," Sam said, knocking on a locked door.

It was opened by another big man, a blond one this time. Were all of these men clones of the Hulk? she wondered hysterically. If his casual clothes were any indication, this one didn't mingle with the public. He wore low-slung jeans and a cotton shirt that was stretched tight across his shoulders. He had truly awesome biceps.

Sam nodded a casual greeting. "Hi, Len. I'm showing Miss Clayton here—" he gestured in her direction "—around the place."

Len stood squarely in the doorway, filling it. "This isn't part of a tour package," he growled.

Sam nodded again, apparently unfazed by the intimidation emanating from the big blond. "Munder's orders," he said cheerfully. "The lady gets to go wherever she wants, and she wants to go *here*."

Len scowled, hesitated, then slowly moved his bulk from the doorway.

Grinning down at her, pleased at the small display of one-upmanship, Sam waved her forward.

Rafe had been right, Dani decided, stepping into the room. Munder did have more—of everything. More monitors, more men, more space, more muscle. Her stomach slowly clenched into one solid knot. What on earth am I doing in here? she wondered miserably.

A quick glance at her watch jolted her from misery to panic. Ten minutes to figure out the system behind all of the monitors!

"Sam," she said determinedly, "tell me how you know what you're doing up here."

"Simple," he said easily, prodding her forward, close enough to the unhappy Len that she could hear him breathing. His heavy puffs of air reminded her of a bull pawing the ground just prior to rampaging across a field, trampling anything in sight.

Wincing at the thought, she moved a step nearer Sam. "So tell me," she urged, taking another peek at her watch. Eight minutes.

Once he explained it, the layout seemed relatively simple. The monitors were arranged in a tight-knit U shape: slots and roulette were covered on the left wall; lounges, offices, corridors and one blank screen at the back; and blackjack and craps tables on the right. The four men in the room constantly scanned the monitors, speaking softly into two-way radios when they spotted anything unusual.

"See?" he demonstrated, flicking switches by a screen at the right. "You can see long distance or get up right next to them."

Dani nodded, blinking as Billy picked up the dice and looked up from the craps table. On the back wall a monitor showed Emily leading an enthusiastic round of applause as Tabitha and Zak finished their act and left the room.

"What are those?" Dani asked, pointing to the empty corridors.

"The back halls we walked through," Sam said. "They lead to the offices. If anyone is fool enough to break into the place, he'll have to come that way."

And it was exactly where Nicholas and Elise would be in—Dani glanced at her wrist—three minutes, counting on her to divert the security force.

"Why is that one blank?" she wondered aloud, nodding at the one dark screen.

"It's the boss's personal room."

"His office?" Dani asked, remembering antlers and glassy-eyed animals.

"Nah." Sam shook his head. "It's where he holds his private games. He's been trying to talk one of the local hotshot gamblers into a poker game for months. The guy's been blackballed in almost every casino in the state, but the boss thinks he can take him."

Cool fingers of apprehension brushed the back of Dani's neck. Before they could get a stranglehold, Sam flipped the switch. The screen blinked to life, displaying a table full of chips, a gently perspiring Jed Munder and a disgustingly handsome, casually alert, expressionless Rafe Sutherland.

Chapter Ten

Rafe sat there with his cowboy hat resting on the back of his head, looking like the devilish gambler in a Western. His shirt was open at the neck and his sleeves were rolled up to his forearms. For all the concern he exhibited, they could have been playing for matchsticks instead of the stacks of chips piled in neat rows before them. He added another handful to the pot and watched, poker-faced, as Munder showed his cards and raked in the pile.

"The boss looks like he's doing okay," Sam commented.

Len looked up at the screen. "Luck's been pretty even for the past four hours."

"Four hours?" Dani looked from one to the other. "Don't they ever get tired?"

"Nope," Len told her with a shake of his head. "This'll probably go on until sometime tomorrow. They feed on adrenaline. A waiter takes in food every few hours, but it'd be worth his head to talk to either of them.''

"Yeah," Sam agreed with a nod. "The boss told me once that if the place catches fire while he's in there to call the fire department, but don't bother him.''

Dani was about to make a pungent comment about compulsive gamblers, when she remembered the time. Good Lord! The shock of seeing Rafe might have just made mincemeat of her carefully constructed schedule, she realized belatedly, frantically raising her wrist. *Thirty seconds.* Taking one last, nervous peek at the empty halls on the screens before her, she turned and deliberately strolled along the left wall.

She stopped midway, finding Earl Dean and Red on one of the screens, staring intently at the roulette wheel, waiting for the ball to slow down and drop into one of the partitions. Billy Bob stood off to the side, teetering on the heels of his cowboy boots, an expression of mild interest on his face. He glanced casually at his watch, looked at the two men and gave a slow nod.

Red lifted an attaché case, supported it on the edge of the table and opened it. It was full of money.

"Sam!" At Dani's urgent tone, all five men turned around. "Look at this! That man has a suitcase of money and he's dumping it all on the table. I think he wants to bet the whole thing!" The men crowded around Dani, staring at the escalating scene. Len picked up a radio and muttered something. A pit boss appeared on camera, looked questioningly at the croupier, listened for a moment, painstakingly helped Red restack the money and urged him away from the table. Before they left, Sam fiddled with a knob and had the camera zoom in.

"Those are hundreds," he said, his brows shooting up as he examined the bills.

Len heaved a disgusted sigh and reached for the radio again. "Some people just don't have any sense." At Dani's look of inquiry, he shook his head and explained. "You don't walk around *anywhere* with a bag of money like that. I'd better get him a guard before someone snatches it."

The other men ambled back to their positions and Dani risked a quick look at the back wall. The monitors showing the hallways were quiet. She closed her eyes in silent gratitude.

Thinking back to Wednesday morning, she remembered how Nicholas had shown them the drawings, explaining that four danger points existed where wide-range cameras covered intersecting corridors. In an ordinary building it wouldn't be a problem. But in a casino, with bright lights and twenty-four-hour surveillance, it was definitely a problem. What he needed was a diversion. Actually, five of them—one final, long one to give him and Elise ten minutes in the accountant's office, where the papers were filed. After that, they'd all be home free. The two of them would slip out into the main casino with the papers in Elise's gaudy tote bag and mingle with the crowd.

All the conspirators had volunteered, but no cohesive plan had developed until Dani hesitantly mentioned viewing Rafe's closed-circuit television at the casino and the card she had from Munder, giving her carte blanche in his place.

That was all Nicholas needed. With the precision of a master tactician, he had shaped his volunteers into a group of commandos, with Dani at the center. Now the score was one down, four to go. Another twenty minutes and it would all be over.

Turning back to examine the monitors before her, Dani zeroed in on the rows of slot machines. Although there was no sound, the feverish activity was obvious. The flashing whirl of plums, oranges, cherries, blinking lights and tumbling coins all added to the excitement. Billy, hands stuffed in his back pockets, turned and watched as Tabitha and Zak appeared at the end of a row. He pulled one hand free, glanced at his wrist and nodded.

Tabitha let go of Zak's hand and spoke to him. He shambled away, coming to a halt behind a plump, frizzy-haired woman playing four machines at once, his eyes flicking from one to another.

Dani giggled at his fascinated expression. "Sam, come watch this," she called, an amused tremor in her voice. "Not all the entertainment is in the lounge," she added as Zak tapped the woman on the shoulder. Sam walked over to join Dani, and four heads swiveled at his crack of laughter.

The woman turned, her nose almost touching Zak's. He grinned ingratiatingly, stretched out a long arm to collect her coins and dropped them in her slack hand. The woman stared, a horrified expression freezing on her face, her eyes rounding until the whites were visible all around the irises. Her open mouth was a dark circle in her face. Zak cocked his head and peered interestedly, seeming to inspect her tonsils. She let out a shriek that sent him reeling back, blinking and steadying himself by clutching a tall, thin man around the waist.

The men clustered around Dani, broad grins creasing their faces until Len shook his head, muttered an oath and reached for the radio. "Who the hell let a monkey in the place?" he asked in a quiet snarl. In the listening silence that followed someone explained that Zak was a celebrity and part of the evening's entertainment.

Tabitha appeared, collected Zak and took him away. Billy melted into the crowd. Dani checked the back monitors again and found the halls quiet and uninhabited. *Two down.*

Wondering how Scanner and Arthur were doing at home, Dani wandered over to the other side of the room. So far it hadn't been bad at all, she decided, trying to locate Bobby Joe. Everything had gone exactly as planned. Billy and his friends were having the time of their lives, and so, presumably, were Nicholas, Elise, Emily and Tabitha. And Dani Clayton? she asked herself. How was she doing? Now that her breath was no longer stuck somewhere down in her lungs, she was higher than a kite. Yes, she admitted, I'm having fun! This is the way it's *supposed* to be: a rush of adrenaline, the ability to think clearly and make instantaneous decisions. It was wonderful!

Looking back at the screens behind her, her gaze settled on Rafe's face. Was that how he felt? she wondered. If it was, he gave no sign. His hat was still tilted at an angle, his mouth, beneath that delicious mustache, relaxed. But his dark, gambler's gaze was totally unreadable. He scooped a large pile of chips toward him with no outward sign of emotion. She decided right there and then that he'd be a dangerous man to play with.

Before she could decide who was winning, she remembered she was still on duty and turned back to look for Bobby Joe's round, amiable face. It was a face that had saved Bobby Joe's neck more than once, Billy had told her. No one could look as innocent as Bobby Joe, especially when he was cooking up a mess of trouble.

Standing a few feet from Bobby Joe, Billy nodded. "Psst! Sam! Come here a minute!"

Dani's agitated hiss drew the eyes of all five men. Len heaved a sigh and muttered something about women, but turned with the rest of them.

"Is it okay to have some cards in your pocket when you play blackjack?" Dani asked.

Len swore and shouldered his way to the front.

"I thought not," she said, her voice creamy with satisfaction.

"Where?" Len asked.

Feeling like Judas, Dani pointed to Bobby Joe. "At least," she backtracked cautiously, "that's what it looked like. He put something in his jacket pocket before he went to the table." She watched as Len picked up the omnipresent radio and snarled to another hapless pit boss.

"What time of the month is it? Is it a full moon?" he demanded, snapping off the radio. "We've had more than our share of loonies tonight."

Dani shrugged, looking over his shoulder to the empty halls pictured on the screens in back. *Three down, one to go.* It was almost anticlimactic to watch a protesting Bobby Joe being led away, especially since she knew nothing would be found in his pockets.

Glancing around, Dani saw that Emily was still handing out awards, Rafe had just lost a big pot, Tabitha was leading Zak by the hand and Billy, Red and Earl Dean had met at the craps table. Billy had the dice and was surrounded by a large crowd.

"I don't believe it!" she gasped, pointing at one of the screens.

Len groaned. "Now what?"

Sam came over and looked, his gaze following her pointed finger. Shaking his head, he said, "You really hit the jackpot tonight. When I worked here, nothing ever happened."

The three others craned their necks to see what was going on.

"There!" she exclaimed, pointing to Red. "That's the man with the caseful of money. He's trying to get it out again." And a guard was trying to stop him. The two men tugged until the case opened and packets of one-hundred-dollar bills fell to the floor. Bodies, coming from all directions, followed them.

Dani switched her gaze from the riot on the center screen to the back wall. She couldn't tell if Rafe was winning or losing, but all the halls were clear. And by now Nicholas and Elise were in the offices, some-where—she glanced up at two monitors in the upper left corner—in there. And now all she had to do was keep the five men from spotting any movement in that area.

All? Her sense of euphoria seemed to shrivel and drain out her toes. She must be crazy! Ten minutes suddenly stretched out to hours. Closing her eyes, afraid that her gaze would draw those of the men, Dani took in a deep, ragged breath.

"What the hell?" Len's voice boomed out close behind her.

Terror held her frozen for a moment. Afraid to open her eyes, afraid not to, Dani squinted through her lashes—and stared in sheer, utter disbelief. The black-and-white screens were flickering, dimming, dying out and slowly returning to life. Not all at once, she noted absently. There was no apparent pattern, but all three walls were afflicted with the random dying and rebirth. In all the confusion, none of the men seemed to notice that the two upper left monitors remained dark.

"I don't give a damn what your readings say," Len roared into a telephone. "Get us on the standby generator! If we lose any more power, I'll personally kick your butt from one end of Carson Street to the other! Now *move*."

God bless all hackers, Dani thought, doing an about-face on the subject. Socks or no socks, the boy was brilliant. She had no doubt at all that Scanner was behind this artistic display. It was precisely the sort of challenge he would appreciate.

Len reached for the telephone again, punching the buttons with such ferocity it was a wonder they didn't crumble under the attack. Dani winced as he bellowed, "What do you *mean*, we're on the alternate power? There are so many lights blinking on and off in this room it looks like Christmas Eve! Get one of your bright boys up here. *Now!*"

The monitor covering Munder's office had remained constant throughout the display. Now, as Dani watched, his door opened and Zak stuck his head in. Finding the room empty, he came in the rest of the way and closed the door behind him. Dani reached out and tugged on Sam's sleeve. "I have a feeling we're in for a show," she murmured, pointing to the screen, when he looked down at her.

Using his long arms and callused knuckles as crutches, Zak swung slowly around the room, coming to a stop when he encountered a particularly bilious-looking moose head. A new black Stetson swung from one broad antler. Extending a long arm and snagging it, he shambled over to a mirror.

Trying on a new hat, Dani knew, was one of the joys of Zak's life. Since he usually stole them, he rarely had the leisure to preen before a mirror, so she wasn't surprised at his anticipatory grin as he eyed his image.

"The boss is gonna have a fit," Sam murmured, watching with a broad smile. "He just bought that hat. Came in as proud as a peacock with it yesterday."

Zak perched it over one eye, then the other. Dissatisfied with the results, he placed it atop his head.

"Mr. Munder obviously has a large head," Dani said, watching as it slid down to Zak's nose.

With one finger applied to the brim, Zak pushed it up until the hat dangled on the back of his head. He edged closer to the mirror until his breath fogged up a round patch, then slowly crossed his eyes.

Even though Dani was accustomed to seeing a cockeyed ape, she still grinned. Sam, after he recovered, let out a chortle. The sound attracted Len.

Len was not amused. "Who the hell let that monkey run loose? And why is he in the boss's office? And what damn fool let him have the boss's hat?" Snatching up the radio, he rapped out an order for someone to attend to an intruder in Mr. Munder's office and went back to tear a few more strips from the maintenance man.

Oblivious of the concern he was causing, Zak left the mirror for greener pastures. Spotting a large gift box of fruit, he stopped to examine it, and the hat once again fell over his eyes. He carefully placed it upside down on the rug. Turning back to the fruit, he peeled a banana and ate it in two bites. Then he carefully extracted oranges, plums, apples and nectarines and lined them up on the edge of the large walnut desk.

Retrieving the hat, he stuffed the top half with the cellophane, grasslike packing material, dropped in a couple of nectarines for good measure, then slammed it back on his head.

"Not bad," Sam said admiringly. "It's a little wobbly, but at least it's staying up."

Zak circled the room, stopping to examine the stuffed animals. He reached up a long arm to tweak the nose of a glittering-eyed deer. When it didn't respond, he gave a shrug and moved along. He finished the circuit at the same time he discovered the camera. Climbing up in a chair to eye it from a closer vantage point, he curled back his lips in a smile that showed all his large, stained teeth.

Dani turned to Sam with a frown of concern. "The man Len sent up to the office won't hurt him, will he?"

"More than likely it'll be a posse. The boss won't take kindly to the fact that someone got in his office."

Dani spun on her heel and approached Len. Pushing down the plunger of the telephone, she cut him off in mid-spate. Ignoring his furious glare, she pointed to the screen and said, "You'd better make sure that no one hurts that animal."

Len's gaze followed the direction of her finger, settling on the monitor just as Zak once more crossed his eyes. He shuddered. "No one's going to miss a simpleminded monkey."

"Your boss sponsored a banquet tonight so he could get some publicity for his new community service program," she reminded him urgently. "He wouldn't like it at all if America's favorite animal star was killed by one of his employees."

Len flung down the receiver with a pungent oath. Striding over to the monitor, he activated the sound. He reached it just as the door was thrown open and two men rushed in. "Don't shoot!" he roared.

The sound, coming from a heretofore silent camera, startled Zak. He whirled around, jumped to the floor, thumped his chest threateningly, curled back his lips and screeched.

The grisly sight was enough to momentarily stun the two men. The second one, obviously deciding that facing down enraged apes did not fall within his job description, edged out the door, slamming it behind him. The other one, made of sterner stuff, raised his pistol just as Zak moved.

Reacting to a pointed gun and the loud noise, Zak did what any Tabitha-trained animal would do. He died. One hand clamped the black hat to his head; the other clutched at his heart as he staggered across the floor.

"Did he shoot?" Len asked Dani in disbelief. "Did the bastard *shoot* him?" he roared.

In the office, the man winced at the noisy roar and looked at his gun questioningly.

Zak groped for the corner of the desk, nectarine juice running down his neck.

"He's bleeding," Len said, staring as a piece of mangled nectarine fell to the floor. "Harry, you damned idiot, his brains are falling out! You shot him—now *help* him!"

Harry, reluctantly approaching the staggering simian, prodded at the pulp on the floor with the toe of his shoe. "Jeez, what a mess," he said in revulsion.

Zak reeled around the room, dropping obnoxious clumps of fruit and packing material, until he finally fell with a thud that shook the floor.

Harry looked at the camera. "What should I do with him?"

"Do with him?" Len choked. "*Fix* him. If you have to, use CPR!"

Harry looked down at Zak.

Zak rolled his eyes back until only the whites could be seen. His lips twitched.

Harry gagged.

The door was thrown open and before Harry could react, Tabitha walked in. "Zak," she scolded, "I couldn't find you anywhere. What are you doing on the floor, and where did you get that hat? Get up from there right now!"

Zak opened one eye, looked at Harry and gave a loud raspberry. Swinging to his feet, he returned the hat to the moose antler, grabbed a handful of packing grass and scrubbed at his head. Tossing the stuff back in the box, he took Tabitha's hand and walked out the door.

In the heavy silence that followed, Len scowled around at the flickering screens. Gradually they steadied, until once again they were all functioning.

All of them, Dani noted. Not a thing moved in the two in the upper left corner. All the halls were empty. On the right, she noticed that Billy and his crew were being escorted out by an armed guard. Emily was wrapping up the banquet and Tabitha was leading Zak outside. Dani searched the left side until she found

Nicholas, wearing a tweed jacket over a dark turtle-neck, with his hand at Elise's waist. She had a bright scarf around her neck and carried a matching tote. By the looks of it, it was heavy.

Touching Sam on the arm, she said quietly, "Thanks for the tour, Sam. I think it's time to go." He nodded amiably and told Len they were leaving. Len scowled and muttered that it was about time.

Taking one last look at Rafe's inscrutable face, Dani walked out the door.

Chapter Eleven

Dani leaned back on the porch swing, pushing it idly with one foot. She was grateful for the early morning silence. The party last night had been long and loud. Champagne, iced down by a confident Nicholas, had been brought out and used to toast all the participants in the night's event. It had been a lengthy process. No one was forgotten. Stemmed crystal glasses were raised to Billy, Earl Dean, Red, Bobby Joe, Emily, Tabitha, Zak, Arthur, Scanner, Nicholas, Elise and Dani. It was only when the diehards started toasting Tabitha's luminaries and Emily's Whalers that Dani excused herself.

Now they were all inside, asleep. The only one missing was Rafe, and she expected him sometime today. Whenever the big game was over. She nudged the floor again with her toe. She would be waiting right here for him.

He was going to ask her to stay. Maybe not today, but he was going to ask her. Could she live with a gambler? The question had kept her awake all night. And now she knew. She couldn't live *without* this particular gorgeous gambler. How it would work out, she didn't know. Only that it would. Somehow.

She had learned something last night, she reflected sleepily, stretching out and tucking a pillow behind her head. Something... very... profound. Rafe had been right. The whole world was a giant casino, and everybody gambled. Billy had bet his last penny that there was oil on his dusty little ranch. Emily, that people cared enough to save the world. Arthur, every time he invested money. Nicholas, at times his very life. Tabitha, that her time spent with animals like Zak would make the world a happier place. And Dani Clayton? Her risks were taken with people. As Rafe said, that was probably the biggest gamble of all.

This was all leading somewhere, she thought hazily, but where? Ah, she remembered. All gambling wasn't bad. There were the good guys and the bad guys. Munder was bad, and Rafe was good. Definitely, she decided, thinking of the warm honey that moved through her body when his mouth covered hers. Not just good—great!

Rafe slid out of the car and straightened his arms in a bone-popping stretch. He took the stairs two at a time, slowing down only when he saw Dani sleeping on the swing. A sense of déjà vu tugged at him as he looked down at her. Only this time, he couldn't wait for her to wake up.

"Dani?" He bent down, sitting on his heels cowboy-style, setting his hat on the floor beside him. "Honey?"

Drowsy hazel eyes opened and smiled into his. Warm arms slid around his neck and a husky voice said, "Hi, I've been waiting for you." Soft lips parted and lifted to his.

"Well," he said softly, just before his smiling mouth touched hers. "If you're asleep, don't wake up until we finish this." One arm slid beneath her shoulders, the other under her knees, and he stood, bringing her up with him. Turning, he sat down on the swing with her in his lap.

"Mmmmm," Dani said with a sigh after a lengthy silence, "that was nice."

"Nice," Rafe agreed lazily, running his hand along the fascinating curves from her knee to her breast. Since she was clad in brief shorts and a halter top, he had access to an intriguing amount of honey-soft skin. His fatigue had disappeared.

Remembering what had caused his weariness, Rafe slowly straightened. There were a few things that needed clearing up, and he preferred to get them out of the way before trying to hammer out their future.

"Dani, about last night. I couldn't see you because I, ah, had an appointment."

Running her fingers over the crisp, dark hair on his arms, she nodded in agreement. "I know. You told me the other day."

"It wasn't exactly an appointment," he clarified, putting his hand over hers to stop the distracting movement of her fingers. "It was more of a card game." He looked down at her, waiting for her expression to change.

"I know," she said calmly.

"Munder had been trying to get me in a game for several months."

She nodded encouragingly.

"But he never had anything I wanted, so I refused."

She nodded again.

"Until this whole thing came up, that is."

She tilted her head questioningly, lifting her other hand to trace the deep crease in his cheek.

"Do you know what I wanted?"

"What did you want?" she asked obediently, her thumb touching the end of his mustache.

"His casino."

Blinking at the casual statement, she repeated, "His casino?"

He nodded.

"He'd never risk losing it," she said with certainty. When he didn't contradict her, she asked, "Would he?"

"With the proper bait."

"Which was?" she asked, beginning to pay attention.

"The Golden Door."

Bracing one hand against his broad shoulder, she demanded, "You mean you two were playing for the casinos?"

"For the controlling interest," he clarified.

"That's one heck of a lot of money," she stated, her trained mind rebelling at the thought of such a wager. "Why would he take such a risk?"

"You gave me the idea," he told her, then grinned at her startled expression.

"I couldn't have. I don't know anything about the man, except that he's a crook."

"And he wants to mingle with the cream of society," he added. "What better place to do it than the Golden Door?"

"My God," she whispered, awed at the enormity of the idea. "Why would *you* take such a risk? You could have lost everything."

He grinned again, genuinely amused at the appalled look on her face. "I told you I was good. Besides, it seemed to be the best way to get him out of the business. Part of the agreement was that he wouldn't open another one in the state."

"But you couldn't *know*," she said, frowning fiercely.

His thumb smoothed away the worried line between her brows. "That's why it's called gambling," he reminded her.

"My God!" She sat up straighter, her eyes widening with horror. "Did you win?"

His crack of laughter and quick hug were enough. She didn't need his "Of course I did."

Dani let out a gusty sigh. "I don't think I could take this kind of pressure very often. Being in love with a gambler can be a little nerve-racking."

Rafe went very still. His eyes met hers and by her anxious expression he knew that she had just taken the biggest gamble of her life. "Dani?" He cleared his throat. "Do you mean it?"

She nodded. "I do, but I have to admit I'm a little scared about the whole thing."

His eyes closed and he drew in a ragged breath. He tugged her against him, wanting all her warmth, her softness, her strength. "I love you," he said tenderly.

"More than you can imagine. Ever since that first night in my office. Does that help?"

"A lot," she said, her lips moving against his throat. "But..."

"But what? You're afraid I'll gamble away your home and hearth?"

"No." She blinked away sudden tears, knowing that he had just given her Sutherlands. "It's just that we're so different."

He raised her chin with a finger and kissed her soft lips. "Not in the things that count," he assured her. "Besides, I turned in my union card after the game ended this morning. I won't be doing anything like that again. I've lost my concentration. I kept thinking about you all evening. I almost had the feeling you were looking over my shoulder."

A rush of delight swept over her, telling her the exact measure of her relief—and masking, just a bit, her feeling of guilt. She would tell him about last night, she promised herself. As soon as she had the right opening.

"What a shame," she lied through her teeth. "I had quite made up my mind to marry a gambler."

"You've got one," he said, shifting so she could lie along the length of him. "The only difference is the stakes. Actually," he admitted, grinning down at her, "I turned my card in several years ago."

Dani narrowed her eyes suspiciously. "What do you mean?"

"I sold the controlling interest of the casino to my mother and bought a ranch."

"The kind with a lot of cows?"

"Cattle, Dani, c-a-t-t-l-e. Not cows."

"The ones that you can see from your window?"

He nodded, his eyes gleaming with amusement.

"And the couple of acres that came with the house?"

His brows rose encouragingly.

"The whole valley where those co—cattle are eating grass, I suppose?"

He nodded and sighed at the same time. "Grazing, honey. Cattle graze."

Dani clenched her fingers and thumped his shoulder with a fist. "Rafe Sutherland, I could murder you! You scared the living daylights out of me. I didn't want to fall in love with a gambler."

"I know. Believe me, the temptation to let you go on believing that I was one was impossible to resist once you turned your nose up at my evil life."

"You were gambling with Elise's share of the casino," Dani pointed out.

"I would have paid her if I lost."

Shifting until his leg lay over hers, he held her with easy strength. "You know what this means, don't you?"

"Yes," she said rashly, "That I won't ever get to watch you in a poker game again."

"It means," he said with characteristic single-mindedness, "that you won't have to go to Munder's tonight."

There was a loaded silence while each of them absorbed the other's words.

"What do you mean, 'again'?" he asked ominously.

Dani's eyes slid away from his face. "Ah, Rafe...I wanted to talk about that. I meant to mention it earlier, but we've been pretty busy," she pointed out with virtuous honesty.

"Damn it to hell, Dani," he snarled, almost dumping her off the swing, "you were there last night, weren't you?"

She closed her eyes in resignation and nodded.

"Where?"

"Well, Billy was sort of floating around, Emily was supervising the banquet, Arthur was home with Scanner, creating havoc with the computer—" she enumerated with precision.

"You, Dani," he interrupted ruthlessly, glaring down at her. "Where were *you*?"

"Up where they keep the closed-circuit TVs," she said baldly, evading his gaze.

"You were locked up in that room with Len Snyder, chief of the goon squad?" His tone implied that since she had escaped death at their hands, he might just do the job himself.

"Not alone," she said quickly. "Sam Farley and three other guys were there."

"That doesn't reassure me," he informed her in no uncertain terms. "They're just more of the same. Perhaps," he said politely, "you'd tell me about the evening?"

Her face lighted up. "Rafe, you would have loved it."

When she finished, he was speechless, torn between fury and the wish that he could have seen it himself. "You told me you were going Saturday," he reminded her. "For that matter, my own mother told me it was Saturday."

"We lied," Dani said calmly.

"If you ever," he began, "do any—"

"Now, Rafe, don't try to coerce me. And don't try to make me promise. When people need my help, I can't say no. And the family is always so pleased to help out.''

He stopped her words with his lips, knowing that if he couldn't stop her, he'd at least be right beside her.

Later, lying spoon fashion on the swing, her body curved contentedly into his, they heard the screen door open. Looking down, they saw a long arm, covered with rusty hair, snake out. Long fingers eased around the brim of Rafe's hat and slid it through the door.

''Damn it,'' Rafe said in mild complaint. ''Am I going to have to put up with that the rest of my life?''

Dani looked up, a smile on her love-softened face. ''It goes with the territory, Mr. Sutherland.''

Epilogue

Dani rolled over in the huge king-size bed. "Are you asleep?"

Rafe's arms tightened around her waist and drew her against him. "Nope. Are you?"

Settling one bare leg between his, she nestled her head on his shoulder, savoring the muscular planes and angles of his body. After three years she still lusted after the man. Positively disgraceful, she thought with a satisfied grin.

"Everything ready for the party?" he asked lazily.

"Um-hmm."

"Want me to do anything besides the usual?"

"Yes. Pry Nicholas away from the casino. Ever since he bought out your part of the business, he never leaves the place."

"Do you suppose it's the business or my mother?"

"Both." She sighed contentedly. "They're so happy together."

Running a strand of her hair across his lips, he murmured, "They'd better be. A second anniversary party is serious business."

"I saw the doctor today."

She could feel his jolt of tension. He worried too much, she worried. About everything. Big things, little things, all the man did was worry about her. Followed her around as if she might disappear from the face of the earth.

"And?" he asked carefully.

She wove her fingers through the crisp mat of hair on his chest. "You will be pleased to know that Daniel is fine. So is Dian. They're six weeks old today and healthy as horses."

"And you?" he asked even more carefully. She had almost died giving birth to the twins. He still woke up in the middle of the night, afraid to reach out, afraid she might not be there.

"I," she said cheerfully, "am terrific. I've been telling you that for days. Now the doctor confirms it. And I plan to prove it. Tonight. Now."

"Honey," he said, capturing her hand as it brushed down past his waist, "what did she say exactly?"

"She said," Dani said precisely, "that you are to quit treating me like spun glass." Her hand escaped from his and continued its journey, stopping at his convulsive movement. "She said that I am a woman and you're a man. And we should act like we know what to do about it."

A half grin tilted his mustache. "Did she now?"

"She did," Dani assured him. With a twist of her body, she rolled over, coming to rest on top of him. Resting her forearms on his chest, her bravado momentarily gone, she whispered, "I've missed you so, Rafe."

He brushed away a tear with his thumb. His hands settled on either side of her head and brought her mouth down to his. "Dear God, Dani," he muttered against her mouth, "I thought you were going to die. Don't ever do that to me again."

"Never," she promised. Later, raising her head from his kiss, she murmured, "About the doctor's advice."

His mustache tilted again as she moved against the velvet hardness of his body. "I don't seem to have much choice in the matter."

"I don't either," she told him with a slight gasp. "I don't think we ever will. It seems to go with the territory, Mr. Sutherland."

COMING NEXT MONTH

#508 ONE OF THE FAMILY—Victoria Glenn
Author Alexandra Reynolds was in L.A. under false pretenses—but that wasn't a problem until she met handsome Mark Conover and fell in love. What would he do when he found out why she was *really* there?

#509 TANGLED TRIUMPHS—Terri Herrington
When consumer advocate Reese Cartwright found a flaw in a product, he did everything he could to bring it to public attention. Only this time, the target was a toy manufactured by Carly Abernathy—the woman he'd never stopped loving.

#510 A MIST ON THE MOUNTAIN—Stella Bagwell
Broken Bow Lake was just what the doctor ordered for Dallas attorney Adam Slade—peace, quiet, and fishing guide Jessie Kincaid. Could a city slicker and a country gal find "happily ever after"?

#511 PERFECT PARTNERS—Jennifer Mikels
Meg Gallagher swore she would never get involved with another cop after her fiancé was killed on duty. But that was before Detective Sergeant Ryan Brady arrived in town. Her head told her to slow down, but her heart was full speed ahead.

#512 NO COMPETITION—Debbie Macomber
Shane Reynolds had long admired Carrie Lockett's art—almost as much as the artist herself. But buying her paintings was easier than getting close to Carrie. Could he convince her that together they could create a masterpiece—of love?

#513 ON RESTLESS WINGS—Mia Maxam
The Red Baron had no business landing his plane in Gloria's pasture and disrupting her solitude—or being so handsome. She wished Major Ross Adams would just fly away...and take her with him.

AVAILABLE THIS MONTH:

ATTRACTIVE, SPACE SAVING BOOK RACK

Display your most prized novels on this handsome and sturdy book rack. The hand-rubbed walnut finish will blend into your library decor with quiet elegance, providing a practical organizer for your favorite hard-or soft-covered books.

Only $9.95

Approximately 16" x 8" when assembled

Assembles in seconds!

To order, rush your name, address and zip code, along with a check or money order for $10.70* ($9.95 plus 75¢ postage and handling) payable to *Silhouette Books*.

Silhouette Books
Book Rack Offer
901 Fuhrmann Blvd.
P.O. Box 1325
Buffalo, NY 14269-1325

Offer not available in Canada.

*New York residents add appropriate sales tax.

BKR-2R

All men wanted her,
but only one man would have her.

Her cruel father had intended
Angie to marry a sinister cattle baron twice her age.
No one expected that she would fall in love with his
handsome, pleasure-loving cowboy son.

Theirs was a love no desert storm would quench.

Available in JUNE or reserve your copy for May shipping by sending your name,
address, zip or postal code along with a check or money order for $4.70 (in-
cludes 75 cents postage and handling) payable to Worldwide Library to:

In the U.S.

Worldwide Library
901 Fuhrmann Blvd.
Box 1325
Buffalo, NY 14269-1325
Please specify title with book order.

In Canada

Worldwide Library
P.O. Box 609
Fort Erie, Ontario
L2A 5X3

 WORLDWIDE LIBRARY

STM-1